NORTHERN BLOOD 1

edited by
Martin Edwards

Magna Large Print Books
Long Preston, North Yorkshire,
England.

British Library Cataloguing in Publication Data.

Edwards, Martin edited by
    Northern blood 1.

    A catalogue record for this book is
    available from the British Library

    ISBN 0-7505-1026-9

First published in Great Britain by Didsbury Press Rodcore Ltd., 1992

Copyright © 1992 by Flambard Press

Published in Large Print November, 1996 by arrangement with the copyright holders.

Magna Large Print is an imprint of
Library Magna Books Ltd.
Printed and bound in Great Britain by
T.J. Press (Padstow) Ltd., Cornwall, PL28 8RW.

NORTHERN BLOOD 1

A Sure-Fire Speculation by Robert Barnard first appeared in *Ellery Queen's Mystery Magazine* in June 1992.

The stories by Robert Barnard, Chaz Brenchley, Ann Cleeves, Eileen Dewhurst, Martin Edwards, Reginald Hill, Margaret Lewis, Peter Lewis, Alan McDonald and Stephen Murray are works of fiction. All characters, firms, organisations, businesses and incidents described are imaginary. Any resemblance to any characters and businesses in real life is coincidental.

CONTENTS

FOREWORD

Several years ago, in November 1953, about a dozen authors gathered at the National Liberal Club at the behest of John Creasey. After a brief discussion (the room had to be vacated at 5.30 pm to make way for the politicians), the Crime Writers' Association was formed. Among its stated intentions was the desire 'to enable members to acquire and exchange knowledge of the genre...' and 'to raise the standards of taste and skill therein.'

In order to achieve these aims it was decided members should meet regularly and have the opportunity of listening to speakers with expertise in all aspects of criminology. It soon became apparent however, that with the greater part of an increasing membership living outside London, local 'Chapters' were needed so that those authors could meet more conveniently locally for the same purpose.

Thus were formed the Edinburgh and St Albans chapters, the West Country chapter who usually meet in Bath, the East Anglian chapter who meet in Wymondham, and finally the Northern Chapter. A widespread membership exists in the north—and it is these convivial writers who are responsible for this anthology.

It must not be thought that all has been sweat and toil for the rest of us since 1953. When I joined the CWA in 1985, my first impression, one that abides, was of a bunch of extremely friendly professionals. Eccentric too, perhaps. That evening, a very large author told me of the distressing, irritating habits of his dearest friend and how he was considering the best and most humane method of extermination. He was so deadly serious it was a relief when another explained he was speaking of his cat.

After the combative nature of the business world it was also refreshing to discover that individuality among writers seemed to counter any sense of threat, as usually exists between rivals.

There is constant discussion about the *failings* of others, of course, we're not that saintly! Publishers, agents, critics and the like come under scrutiny, for if a member's current book didn't obtain the approbation it merited, everyone has to lay the blame somewhere! But there is genuine friendship, long and lasting, between many in the CWA.

This anthology of work by the Northern Chapter illustrates in microcosm the many aspects of crime writing today. There is fact as well as fiction, for the CWA embraces both. Among the contributors there is also a winner of our top award, the Gold Dagger, presented in 1990 to Reginald Hill.

When interviewed, we are often asked how we regard 'the golden age' of British crime fiction. To those who think it ended with the death of Agatha Christie, I would suggest we are currently witnessing a renaissance. The genre, especially in this country, has grown and developed enormously over the past two decades. British authors are translated and sold world-wide, television adaptations of their works can be watched every week from here to Tokyo (or even more profitably, from here to San Francisco).

The Crime Writers' Association has grown too, from the original dozen to close on four hundred members. Next year we celebrate our fortieth anniversary. I think our founder, John Creasey, would have been proud. May you continue to enjoy the results of his and our labours in this, our second golden age.

Nancy Livingston

Chairman
Crime Writers' Association

INTRODUCTION

Almost fifty years have passed since Raymond Chandler declared in *The Simple Art of Murder* that 'the only reality the English detection writers knew was the conversational accent of Surbiton and Bognor Regis.' Times and fashions have changed since then, in crime fiction as well as in society at large. Yet it has taken a long time for places like Hartlepool, Huyton and Humberside to gain voices in the genre. This book is the very first collection of fact and fiction to be put together exclusively by crime writers living and working in the North of England.

The Northern Chapter of the Crime Writers' Association is one of the youngest of the informal regional groupings set up by the Association's members. It owes its existence to the enthusiasm of Peter N Walker, who convened the first meeting at the Crown Hotel, Boroughbridge in North Yorkshire on Sunday, 29th November 1987. 'The Few' (as Reginald Hill dubbed the gathering) came from places as far afield as Newcastle on Tyne, Doncaster, Goole and Wirral—an area which is larger than Wales.

Since then, the Northern Chapter has gone from strength to strength. In the last five years it has organised national CWA conferences at Scarborough and Durham and it has held a weekend symposium in Spring for the last two years, first at Rosedale Abbey in Yorkshire and then at Grasmere. A growing number of writers have attended; apart from the contributors to this volume, the regulars include Meg Elizabeth Atkins and Gwen Moffat.

Northern crime writing has now firmly established its own identity, without needing to delineate a precise geographical boundary. Like an elephant, the North is difficult to describe, but most people recognise it when they encounter it. That said, the region's geography does confuse some outsiders, including a number of eminent figures in the world of crime. In their enjoyable, though idiosyncratic, compilation *A Catalogue of Crime,* Jacques Barzun and Wendell Hertig Taylor transported Knutsford, the Cheshire town of my birth and the model for Elizabeth Gaskell's *Cranford,* across the sea to Ireland, while the compilers of *The Murderers' Who's Who* shifted Gorse Hall, scene of one of history's most remarkable unsolved crimes, from Cheshire to Yorkshire.

England's supposed 'North-South divide' is surely much exaggerated. No sensible analysis of the distinctions that un-doubtedly exist within English society can be substantiated by drawing a crude imaginary line across the country. Yet, for whatever reason, the North has not traditionally been associated with crime fiction. This is surprising, not least because so many of the classic cases of real life have occurred in the region. The Gorse Hall mystery, for instance, is remarkable in that on two separate occasions the police believed they had apprehended the man who stabbed George Harry Storrs. On each occasion the supposed culprit was tried—and acquitted. The mystery continues to baffle eminent criminologists.

Even more puzzling were the two most celebrated cases to have arisen in Liverpool. In 1889, Florence Maybrick was convicted of murder following the death of her husband from arsenic poisoning. She received the death sentence and had the disquieting experience, whilst in prison, of hearing the sound of the construction of her own gallows. A huge public outcry on both sides of the Atlantic led to her sentence being commuted to life imprisonment; in the end she served fifteen years and after her release she emigrated to her native United States where she died in 1941 at the age of 76.

The case fascinated Chandler, who

meticulously listed points for and against the proposition that Florence was guilty. But he decided not to develop his researches further; as he remarked, with much truth, "Nobody ever writes a book about a famous case to prove that the jury brought in the right verdict." The ingredients of the case have naturally attracted the interest of novelists, with sparkling results in Anthony Berkeley's *The Wychford Poisoning Case* and Joseph Shearing's *Airing In A Closed Carriage*.

Chandler was also intrigued by the Wallace case. A mild-mannered insurance agent, William Herbert Wallace, was convicted of the savage murder of his wife; his alibi was based on an unlikely-sounding story that at the time of the murder he had been lured to a false address by a telephone caller who gave his name as 'R.M Qualtrough'. Wallace was found guilty and sentenced to death; although his appeal against conviction succeeded, he died soon afterwards. This mystery, too, has been turned into fiction, in John Hutton's superb *22 Herriott Street*.

Over the years, many other dramatic cases have occurred in the North. For example, Dr Buck Ruxton, who killed his wife and her maid, practised in Lancaster; the forensic detective work which led to the identification of the victims' bodies was masterly. The North East saw the strange case of Evelyn Foster, victim of a bizarre car fire in 1931; there is continuing debate as to whether she was murdered or killed herself accidentally in the process of setting her car ablaze in order to make an insurance claim. In Durham Prison, almost half a century earlier, Mary Ann Cotton was hanged after being convicted of the murder of her stepson. No fewer than 21 people close to her had died during the previous two decades and she is suspected of having committed perhaps fifteen murders in all—a tally which would make her one of the most prolific, as well as one of the earliest, of serial killers.

The North has in the past thirty years seen even more horrific multiple murders. Ian Brady and Myra Hindley buried their tragic victims on the bleak moors north of Manchester. Across the Pennines, Peter Sutcliffe committed thirteen murders over a five year period before the police, who had interviewed him several times during the course of their enquiries, finally identified him as 'the Yorkshire Ripper'.

Nevertheless, it is only in recent times that crime novels have regularly been set in the North. Perhaps this illustrates the traditional gulf between crime fiction and reality. In addition, Southern settings were those with which pre-eminent writers such as Sir Arthur Conan Doyle, Agatha Christie, Dorothy L Sayers, Michael Innes and Edmund Crispin were most familiar. True, Sherlock Holmes ventured as far as Derbyshire in *The Priory School* and Father Brown popped up in Scarborough in *The Absence of Mr Glass*. And every now and then a shady character would make his way to Liverpool, with a view no doubt to fleeing by ship to the New World. In *The Murder of Roger Ackroyd,* Hercule Poirot made a rare journey to Liverpool, but Christie did not attempt to characterise the city. Sayers set much of *Clouds of Witness* in Yorkshire, but few mysteries of the Golden Age of crime fiction between the Wars took place in cities such as Manchester, Bradford or Leeds.

The picture began to change after the Second World War. E.C.R Lorac (the pseudonym concealed the identity of Edith Caroline Rivett) set several of her sturdy mysteries in the Lake District and the Lune Valley. An excellent example is *Crook O'Lune* and another of her stories depends for its solution on knowledge of a safe pathway across Morecambe Bay. Her books, once very popular, are overdue for a revival.

While Lorac skilfully evoked the Northern countryside, Maurice Procter, author of books such as *Hell Is A City*, captured the atmosphere of the gritty urban North in his police procedurals. A similar concern for authenticity marked the work of a later writer, John Wainwright. Like Procter, he was once a policeman and continues to write to this day.

A number of very good novels with a Northern background began to appear in the sixties. One of the best was *The Massingham Affair* by Edward Grierson, a lawyer-author whose few novels are well worth seeking out. The story is set on the Northumberland moors and has a real life basis in the Edlingham Burglary of the late nineteenth century. Stanley Hyland, another crime novelist whose career was regrettably brief, provided a splendid picture of a West Riding mill town in *Green Grow The Tresses-O*, his last novel, which appeared in 1965.

The baton then passed to writers such as John Buxton Hilton, who located both contemporary police investigations and historical crime novels in Derbyshire.

Soon, the trickle of Northern crime novels became a flood. Yorkshire is marvellously realised in Reginald Hill's award-winning 'Dalziel and Pascoe' series. *Under World* deserves special mention for its sensitive depiction of a mining community in the aftermath of the disastrous national strike of 1984-85. Several of his non-series books also derive strength from their northern setting. *Fell of Dark,* the first novel he wrote (although the second published), is a lively thriller about the misadventures of a fell-walker in the Lake District. *Death Of A Dormouse,* a thriller published under his pen-name Patrick Ruell, is an enjoyable account of a Yorkshire widow's investigations into her late husband's secret life.

Robert Barnard, an Essex man by birth but a Leodiensian by adoption, also enjoys an international reputation for witty and well-plotted crime stories, which have earned no fewer than four Edgar award nominations. Hexton-on-Weir in *The Disposal Of The Living* is the Yorkshire town of Richmond in fictional disguise; it is portrayed with rich comedy. The tone of *A City of Strangers* is darker. The titular city of Sleate (perhaps a blend of Leeds and Bradford) is so convincingly described that it becomes one of the book's main characters.

Many of the other members of the Northern Chapter also draw upon their own localities for inspiration. Barbara Whitehead, for instance, has now published four novels in her York Cycle of Mysteries and Peter N Walker, a modern successor to Maurice Procter, sets crime stories, as well as his televised 'Constable' books, in his native region. Ann Cleeves' series featuring Inspector Ramsay and Chaz Brenchley's novel *The Garden* capture the atmosphere of the North East, whilst Alan McDonald and I have our detectives investigating crimes in Merseyside.

When the CWA decided to hold its 1992 conference in Durham, the Northern Chapter decided to celebrate by putting together a collection of stories and non-fiction pieces, each with a Northern element (sometimes peripheral, sometimes central) and a criminal theme.

An enterprising local publisher, Patrick Quinn, was keen to take the book on, but we realised that if it were to be available by the time of the Durham conference, time was, to use the legal phrase, of the essence.

In the event, both authors and publisher responded splendidly to the challenge. Everyone was keen to show that crime writing in the North has never been healthier than it is today. Rather than take the easy course of digging into the vaults for old material, we decided to be original. None of the pieces in this collection has ever been published in the UK before, either in book form or in a magazine.

The sheer diversity of the contents is

striking. We offer a humorous twist-in-the-tail story; a shocking chiller; a journey into the past; a contemporary police investigation; an amateur sleuth's detection with echoes of one or two famous fictional crimes; a story with a supernatural element; a macabre tale of life and death in academe; a weird comedy; a tough urban thriller; and a rural mystery. The non-fiction contributions are as varied. Alan Sewart re-examines a 1920s murder in which he had a personal interest. Douglas Wynn investigates a 1938 case which arguably resulted in a miscarriage of justice. Peter Walker describes a life-or-death manhunt with which he became involved. Barbara Whitehead looks at the connection between wills and crime fiction, whilst Andrew Gardner explains how his local background has influenced his work.

We have taken the opportunity to experiment. Alan Sewart, Peter Walker and Barbara Whitehead are perhaps best known as novelists, but here they stick to hard facts. Conversely, Margaret and Peter Lewis are biographers and critics who are now trying their hands at fiction. Ann Cleeves and I have tested the series detectives of our novels in the short-story form for the first time. Several contributors—including, remarkably, Eileen Dewhurst, whose crime novels have been enjoyed by an appreciative readership on both sides of the Atlantic for more than a decade—had not previously published short crime stories.

I would like to thank all the contributors, as well as Nancy Livingston and Patrick Quinn, Elaine Scanlan and their colleagues at Didsbury Press, for their hard and rapid work. I believe that the result of their endeavours is a book which will entertain all those who share our fascination with crime in the North.

Martin Edwards

Editor

1

A Sure-Fire Speculation
by
ROBERT BARNARD

'Who are you going to the YCs' dance with?' Jennifer Daly was asked by her friend Sharon as they stood in the queue at a sandwich bar one lunchtime.

The Young Conservatives' dances were about the only activity in Felton, a small Derbyshire town not very far from Derby itself. Going to the dances did not imply conservatism, or even youth: it was just a way of showing you were alive. Jennifer Daley certainly was alive—blonde, cool and just twenty-one, though there were very few people who could say they knew her well.

'Well, don't say anything yet, because he doesn't know: I'm going with Simon Slocum.'

'Simon Slocum? But he's dull as ditchwater!'

'Yes, he is... I'm going to marry him.'

'You're what?'

'I'm going to marry him.'

'You mean you're engaged?'

'No, I mean when he asks me I'm going to say yes.'

By now they were outside in the street and well away from any listening ears.

'How do you know he's going to ask you?' Sharon said, thinking that Jennifer was showing a rare flight of imagination.

'Signs... I've been working on him.'

'But why are you going to marry him? You said yourself he's as dull as ditchwater.'

Jennifer considered how best to put it.

'Somehow or other I don't seem to think like other girls. The whole romantic thing has passed me by. When other people get warm feelings I just think: "How silly!" I'm a practical person, and I just take the practicalities into account.'

'What do you mean by practicalities?'

'Home, income, secure future, that sort of thing.'

'But Simon Slocum is no great catch by those lights. He's just a bank clerk in Derby.'

'Ah, but you see, he has Great Expectations.'

'Who from? His father's a retired policeman.'

'An uncle. His mother's eldest brother. Very rich. Lives in a very grand house in the centre of Buxton.'

'But Jenny, you can't marry him relying on his inheriting that money! It's too sordid! Anyway, he could change his mind, this uncle, and make a new will. You'd be reduced to courting his favour, maybe for years and years till he died.'

'Oh no he couldn't, and oh no we wouldn't.'

'What do you mean?'

'He has Alzheimer's Disease. He's not mentally competent to make a new will. Alzheimer's is irreversible. He doesn't recognise anyone any more. Simon has stopped going up there to see him. We'd just sit around waiting to collect.'

'Are you *sure* of this, Jenny?'

'Oh yes, quite sure. The woman who nurses him is a friend of my mother's. Told us about it in a letter. That's how I came to think of Simon like that.'

'Well, but you *are* the practical one!'

But Jenny's friend, in her heart, was using very much harsher words than "practical".

In the short term Jenny's plans worked out beautifully. At the Young Conservatives' dance she gave Simon the sort of attention he was not used to getting from girls in Fenton. She flattered him, but in a subtle, indirect way, because although she thought him a bore she did not think him a fool. When they kissed goodnight, coolly, she

29

told him to call her again soon. Within a fortnight they had been to the cinema twice, to a pub quiz, a race meeting at York, and a talk on the money supply. Jenny's mother told her neighbours that her daughter's new boyfriend was quiet but ever so nice, and told her friends that he was nice but ever so quiet. She thought in her heart that he was the sort of young man you could never get really close to. Jennifer herself had no such doubts. As soon as the topic of marriage came up she made it clear that that was in her mind too. As soon as they were formally engaged she told Simon that she did not believe in long engagements.

'I don't want a slap-bang wedding,' she said. 'I mean, it's like showing off, isn't it, and I'm not that kind. I want a church wedding, but not *too* church.'

She had made it clear from the beginning that she thought sex was for after the wedding, and Simon had said 'Oh, absolutely.' Jenny was Church of England, and Simon said he was too, though in his case it was a bit nominal. Jenny took him along to her local church for the three Sundays before the wedding, and he fitted in very well there. Most of the young men who went to the church were a bit dull too. Jenny would quite happily have married any of them, if he had happened to have an elderly uncle with Alzheimer's Disease and a will already made in his favour.

Jenny's first surprise came on the honeymoon, which was spent in Torquay. Jenny had experimented with sex in her teens and had found that it was something that she could take or leave—certainly she had realised that it did not do for her what it apparently did for so many people. In the hotel in Torquay she discovered that her new husband was sexually experienced to an extent, and in ways, she had never dreamt of. They had not been married two days before he was urging her to try things she had never remotely contemplated—had hardly, indeed, heard mentioned.

'But I don't want to. I think that's disgusting.'

'Try it.'

'I don't want to.'

'You can't know what you want till you try it.'

And afterwards, when she said bitterly that she had found the experience loathsome, he had said: 'Keep on trying. You'll get used to it.'

Jenny felt aggrieved. It was so unfair—that someone who was so dull out of bed should not prove to be equally dull in it. Nor had she expected that her wishes, her preferences, should be so completely set aside. She had expected, in fact, to be the dominant partner. By the end of her honeymoon she was participating in bondage rituals.

'Where did you *learn* all this?' she cried dispiritedly. 'Where did you learn to *want* this sort of thing?'

'There's a very nice woman in Buxton,' Simon said. 'I used to go there to visit my uncle. She taught me all I know.'

To be fair, Simon asked her to do all sorts of things to him, as well as wanting to inflict them on her. But when she tried he told her she was about as convincing as an extra in an Australian soap. So she preferred to be the passive recipient rather than the active player.

By the end of the honeymoon Jenny had decided that 'all that' (as she put it in her own mind) was very silly and unnecessary, but that she could put up with it. So long as it went no further than it had done.

They had rented as their first home a nice little flat in Fenton. Jenny worked in a hairdresser's, and with both their wages they could afford it, and a car and an occasional night out. They set to work to redecorate the flat, with their landlord's approval. It would make the place more like theirs, set their stamp on it. Simon's stamp, if he had been allowed his way, would have been very faint indeed, but

Jenny had ideas of her own, and Simon let her have her way.

'That's the woman's prerogative,' he said, as he also did over such things as food and furniture. The implication, Jenny understood, was that there were other things that were the man's prerogative, and he intended to assert it.

The question of Simon's uncle came up one Saturday, when they were redecorating the bedroom.

'Buying a house will have to wait until uncle dies,' said Simon, slapping paint on to the ceiling. 'But of course you know about him, don't you? Mrs Mackenzie is a friend of your mother's.'

So he had known all along! Known—or at least suspected—that she had married him for his expectations. And had gone along with it. Jenny felt her cheeks burn. She was cutting wallpaper with a sharp-edged tool, and she tried to keep her voice calm as she replied: 'Shouldn't we go and visit him?'

'What's the point? The poor old bugger doesn't know me—doesn't know Mrs Mackenzie, doesn't know anybody.'

That night Simon really hurt her for the first time. He tugged violently and repeatedly at her hair during lovemaking, though by the end she was screaming for him to stop.

'Don't do that. It hurt like hell,' she said afterwards.

'Goes with the territory,' said Simon, shrugging.

It was clear to Jennifer now that her plans had gone horribly wrong. What made it worse was the fact that she had no-one to discuss things with. Her best friend had been the recipient of her confidences before marriage, and had been very cool since. To confess how hideously she had miscalculated would be too humiliating for words. Her mother had never been a confidante, and Jenny shied away from consulting a solicitor. After all, what she wanted to know was whether, if she separated from Simon before he inherited, she would forfeit all rights to the old man's lucre when he died. It was not only that she would seem a money-grubber—she could bear that. But it would probably come out and weigh against her should she decide to murder Simon.

She had come to no conclusions on that score. She was pretty sure that if she divorced him when he had become rich she would be entitled to half the conjugal assets. If she—somehow—murdered him and was not charged, she would get the lot. Half with no risk, the lot with considerable risk. On the other hand, with his tastes, murder could easily be made to look like self-defence. He had not yet begun to play nasty games with knives, but the way he fingered with relish the cutting edge of the carving knife at Sunday lunchtime suggested that it was only a matter of time before he did.

She determined to wait, fortified by a letter to Simon from her mother's friend. 'It pains me to have to tell you that your uncle appears to be sinking fast.'

The only sensible thing to do, Jenny concluded, was to grit her teeth and bear it.

The end of the old gentleman came on a lovely Spring morning in late April, and was announced in a telephone call from Mrs Mackenzie, his nurse. They drove up to Buxton, and Simon proved surprisingly adept at making funeral arrangements. 'I should be,' he said, when they were alone in their room at the Old Hall Hotel. 'I've had long enough to prepare for this.' They rang around to all the relatives Simon could think of, and thus ensured that there was a respectable gathering in the church and at the cold collation with wine that took place in the old man's substantial stone residence afterwards. Simon's parents did not come. They had always been, in Jenny's view, cold to her—and indeed to Simon himself. Now she decided they resented his inheriting his uncle's money.

Mrs Mackenzie, whom Jenny had not seen since she was a child, took them to her substantial bosom and said: 'It was a merciful end to suffering.' But Jenny took care not to catch her eye later during the course of the funeral get-together: she might give her a knowing look, or even a wink, suggesting that she understood her own part in the making of Jenny's marriage to Simon.

The solicitor, visited next morning, was very encouraging. The will had been made ten years before, when Simon's Uncle Albert was running his own business and sat on the Buxton Council. There was no question he was in sound mind when he made it. In a couple of months or so probate would be declared and the estate would be Simon's absolutely. It would be a very considerable estate, and Simon would be set up comfortably for life. Meanwhile there was nothing to stop Simon putting the house on the market, and if they wanted some money in advance, no doubt his uncle's bank...

'Oh no,' said Simon, rather to Jenny's disappointment. 'We're very quiet people. We can wait.'

He rang Mrs Mackenzie before they left and said that when probate was declared he would be showing his gratitude. He realised that by the time she came to minister to his uncle, the old man was beyond recognising her services. Jenny thought this unnecessary: she had been well paid, and would have no difficulty finding similar work in Buxton. But she did not say so. She was a little uncertain how the access of wealth would affect Simon. In any case he would consider such questions the man's prerogative.

Simon took to wealth, in fact, with modest dash. As soon as they were home he took Jenny to order a Daimler, to take delivery in three months' time. He consulted her studiously as to colour and upholstery, while reserving decisions on mechanical matters to himself.

They started to look at good property in the Felton area and the countryside around. Any Old Rectory or substantial Victorian residence that came on the market, they would go along to the Estate Agent's and get an order to view. Soon they were being sent details of the more expensive properties as they were put up for sale. They had made it clear they wanted something large, or in some other way prestige-building.

'It has to be detached,' Simon insisted. 'We can't have neighbours overhearing us.'

He started dressing well, and encouraged Jenny to open up an account with the most prestigious Derby dress shop. They ate out a lot and Simon got a Diners' Club Card. They talked a lot about their first really expensive holiday.

'The place I've always fancied is South America,' said Simon. 'It's one of the last places left in the world with this tang of danger, this tension, this edge. Anything can happen in those countries—they're not safe, stable, cosy places like the rest of the world has become.'

'I don't think I'd fancy it at all,' said Jenny, and in the end they booked a holiday at an expensive but unobtrusive hotel in Nice.

Jenny had hoped that having all that money to spend, at least in anticipation, would take the edge off Simon's sexual appetites. It did not. He became more inventive, and seemed to get even greater pleasure from her distress and pain. But still he did not resort to knives, or to any other implements that could be used against him fatally. Jenny didn't know whether to be sorry or relieved. A knife was a two-edged weapon, and the casualty could so easily be herself rather than Simon. She reconciled herself to making do with a half-share.

Simon was informed by the solicitor in Buxton when probate was granted. He didn't ask Jenny whether she wanted to come with him when he went up to deal with various formalities and to complete the sale of his uncle's house. Jenny didn't offer to come either. She was preparing, though only psychologically, for the end of her marriage. A few days after he got back, a week at most, she would dress after one of his horrible sessions and go down to the police station with the marks still on her.

'Go into Ellison and Hanley's and say we'll complete purchase of the Merriton property as soon as I get back from Buxton,' Simon said before he drove off.

She wondered whether to bother. Simon would hardly be able to afford it when she left him, with half his property and money under threat. Still, it would embarrass him acutely, going round and cancelling all his expensive near-acquisitions. So she did as she had been told.

He said he thought all the business details would take about three days. When he didn't come home then she didn't worry, nor did she try to ring him at his hotel: she wasn't that sort of wife, and it wasn't that sort of marriage. In fact it was five days before she got Simon's postcard, posted second-class from Manchester Airport:

'We're off to Venezuela, and we'll be settling in some exciting, violent country with no inconvenient treaties with Great

Britain. It was a pleasure torturing you all those months. Did you really think I'd let you get your hands on my money? And you *should* have realised that the woman in Buxton who taught me all I know was Mrs Mackenzie. Nurses, you know, are connoisseurs of pain.'

2

A Terrible Prospect of Bridges
by
CHAZ BRENCHLEY

I don't think there's even a word for what I've got. There are other words, of course, people offer me those, but mostly they don't come close. Hydrophobia, for instance, that's a favourite; but that's different, that's rabies. That way madness lies.

It's not water I'm afraid of, no. I'll drink it, wash in it, I'll even go swimming if it's an old-fashioned pool with no wave-machine and preferably no crowds, no happy families splashing in the shallows. But count me among the witches and the spirits, we can none of us cross running water. I can't bear to walk across a bridge.

There are currently eight bridges over the Tyne at Newcastle, eight and counting. Six I can see from my window.

If you drove west from here—I don't, I

don't drive; but if you do, if you did—you could go some way without ever crossing a bridge. You could go quite far enough, at any rate: to where two villages have almost the same name, and are divided only by a wooded valley, and a stream.

You could park in either one, it doesn't matter. There should be plenty of space for cars, there used to be; and both have good pubs, or used to.

But the pub would be for later, after the walk. You'd go on a Sunday, if you had any sense; go nice and easy and relaxed, no hurry. There really isn't any hurry now.

So you'd go, you'd park, you'd lock the car because that's your habit, even in the heart of the country; then you'd look for the footpath that takes you down into the valley, into the wood. At one end it starts in a churchyard, at the other by a barn. But it's still the same path, it would still get you there, whichever way you came.

Fields and stiles, cowpats and mud: you've walked in the country before, you'd know what to expect. A little of that, and then the trees and the path plunging steeply between them. Down you'd go, being careful not to slip; wouldn't want a fall down here, wouldn't want to start a landslide.

Believe me, you wouldn't. Never know what you might uncover.

42

Finally you'd come to the stream, and the settlement; and this would be what you'd come for, maybe. If you'd heard the story.

You'd cross the stream if you were on the wrong side of it, if that was the way you'd come; and you'd notice that there used to be a bridge over, and that there isn't any more. These days, you have to use the stones. It wouldn't be a problem, probably; most people don't find it hard. But even so, you might glance at the wooden uprights still standing firm in the bed of the stream, you might wonder what happened to the bridge across, and why it hasn't been rebuilt.

But then you'd be on the other side, safely over and not even a wet foot to show for it; the stones are solid as any bridge and almost as easy to walk on. And then, all about you, you'd see the settlement.

It was abandoned, of course, a long time ago, and no doubt it shows. Myself, I haven't been back in twenty years; things will be different now. Someone might even have rebuilt the bridge, though I wouldn't have thought so. I wouldn't have thought they would dare.

Anyway, what you'd see is the relics, the remains of a community that built itself around one man's vision, sustained itself as long as that vision lasted and died when the vision died. Twenty years ago it died, and what you'd see is the bones, only the bones.

Skeletal huts you'd see, for sure: rotting wooden walls, fallen roofs. Hearths and chimneys still surviving, perhaps, where they were stone-built, left to point like accusing fingers at the uninterested sky. Some were more ambitious, proper houses, you couldn't call them huts; but they were wood too, they needed their upkeep and won't have received it, they'll be gone like the meanest hovel. Some fallen to the weather, one or two burnt out, I imagine, by accident or design.

I imagine it quite often, how that clearing must look now. Sometimes I think that I may be the only one left who remembers it as it was, in its last casual and heedless days of life; and how I envy the others, all those fortunates whom I suppose to have forgotten, to have trained their minds not to recall it.

I try to train mine by picturing the bones, only the bones with no life in them. And I fail, again and again I fail. Reality is not so easy to cast out.

These days I live freelance and alone and always moving, but never moving far. At the moment my flat overlooks the Tyne, but it might as easily be the Tees or the Wear, or any smaller river. I have to gaze at water, that I dare not stand above.

I am a musician and an artist, occasionally a writer. I have been other things: a baker, a cook, partner in a vegetarian café, sole proprietor of a wholefood shop. Always on the side of the angels, you'll notice, never in the pocket of the establishment. And, of course, always moving on. But never far.

I am known now as Thomas Woodson, but that is not my name. I think it a clever, if a bitter choice. This much at least you can say for certain about my haphazard life: that the man I am, the man I have become was born in that hidden clearing, among the trees and the secrets of that wood.

The Thomas of those days, who was not called Woodson—the man I still long, I still yearn to be—was a tall and vigorous man, often solemn and as often laughing. He saw visions and dreamed dreams, and he believed passionately that what was dreamed could be made real by faith and works together, by intellectual rigour and the body's dedicated labour.

You could call him a messiah, I suppose, on a small scale. A kitchen ecclesiast. He had all the qualifications: he had charisma and he had disciples, both something to

45

say and a way to make people listen. Above all he had the will, the drive, the urge to evangelise. He saw the world very clearly as it was, and he wanted to change it.

In his own way, though, as with everything. He wanted to do it all his own way.

'I'm not going to preach on street corners,' he said time and time again, till he was weary of saying it. 'We've built our mousetrap, and it's better than anyone else's; let the world come to us. Just let them see what we've done, and then we'll trap 'em.' With a grin and a resounding clap of the hands, perhaps a glance around at his little, hopeful paradise.

Because what he'd done, of course, was just what all messiahs mean to do, on whatever scale they can manage.

He'd set his people free.

I find it hard now, impossibly hard to explain how it was in those days, how it felt. New friends always ask: 'Thomas,' they say, 'I don't understand. How could you do that? How could you just lead thirty people off into the wilderness that way, why would they do it? What were you all trying to achieve?'

I don't have an answer, there never was any answer except the thing itself, the settlement as it was; but the settlement is dead now, and so there is no answer any more.

In those days, of course, it was the question that didn't seem to make sense. We knew who we were and what we had; and when journalists asked us where the settlement was going, what we were aiming at, there was nothing to do but laugh. We weren't going anywhere, we were here, we'd arrived. This was forever, our little company in the woods.

People are more cynical today, they have to be, it's the spirit of the age; but I don't think we were naïve even then, it's only cynicism that says so. We had hope, that was all, we had dreams. That was the fashion, that was the culture, the milieu we moved in; and one must needs be fashionable, then as now.

Thomas (and I must, I will still write of him in that way, as someone separated from myself; there's been a lot of water under the bridge since then, and I am not he), Thomas had two women at the settlement, to share his house and his bed and his dreams. Two wives, in all honesty, though there were no certificates of marriage and not a wedding-ring between them.

Two wives, but only one child: a curious, amiable little boy who probably didn't know which his mother was and certainly showed no signs of caring. He was quite happy to share himself between them.

There were other post-hippy colonies, of course, in other places, and most of those were teeming with children; but not this one. Thomas said children were to be cherished when they came, but not hungered for. Human greed, he said, was the one great danger to this planet; and greed for children was the worst, the most immoral and the most dangerous. We were breeding ourselves out of existence, he said. We all had a responsibility to the future; moderation couldn't be legislated for, it had to be an individual decision individually policed.

He and his household were the example, the living precept, and his disciples were all responsible people, or they wouldn't have been there. A couple of the older men had families from an earlier existence, pre-Thomas; but they'd left wives and children both, to live this enclosed and responsible life. So little Paul found himself the only child in a community of tender adults, flourished under their mutual care and no doubt thought the entire world like that.

And never had the chance to learn otherwise, because that was a bridge to cross when he came to it, and Paul never got that far.

I only have new friends, so they're always asking questions, and the questions are always more or less the same. Couched in other language, perhaps, or the emphasis altered, but that's all the difference. One of the favourites might come as, 'The rest of your community, Thomas—what happened to them, are you still in touch?' or it might be, 'How can you *bear* it, being alone with so much to carry? How do you survive that?'

It's still the same question, underneath; and it's usually the young who ask it, having no experience or understanding of solitude, seeing perhaps the first possibility of it in my own great change from that to this, and being afraid.

I tell them no, I'm not in touch with any of the others. A few must be dead by now, and the rest are scattered. Returned to the world or else still in flight from it, dancing to a different drummer; and no, I don't worry about them, how could I? I barely wonder. We can only ever truly care about our own lives, about what touches us; and they are gone from me.

Or I answer the other way, if that's how they ask it. There are some things, I tell them, that it's easier to carry alone.

So Thomas had two wives, one son and a community of seekers. But he had a brother, too. He had Stephen; and Stephen was there from the start. Stephen built the houses.

He was the practical one, converting vision to reality. A *community*, his brother said, *somewhere among trees. A long walk from the city,* Thomas said; and Stephen found the place. *Shelter,* Thomas said, standing in the clearing, looking round. *We'll need shelter, more than tents. We've got a baby coming, and the summer's on the turn.* So Stephen lived there first, alone in a bender while he built the first rough shelters. After that he had help, Thomas and the disciples working willingly under his direction as he got more ambitious on their behalf, and his huts turned to houses; but he was still very much the builder, the man who could make things happen. A man of his hands, always.

So Stephen gave them shelter, and Thomas gave them hope; and they all lived happily ever after, until the end came and all hope died, all shelter proved itself illusion.

But who were they, these communards, these settlers? These disciples?

Well, there were the inevitable hippies, left over from their golden age. There were men and women who'd had one life already, and failed with it. Among the younger people there were student drop-outs and druggies and graduates who weren't ready to tackle the unlimited world, who still wanted to live within someone else's definition.

They were a mixed bag, in other words, a curious assortment. But they all had this much in common, that they believed in Thomas. He wrote their gospels for them, he paved their path to heaven; and they were all prepared to work, to keep it so.

Another of those questions that people always ask came up again last week. I've been teaching an art class for the WEA, and I had a few of them back for drinks afterwards, my newest circle of friends; and one of the lads, he's barely in his twenties yet, he said, 'So you had them two girls, Thomas—but what about the others? Was it all like that, was it, what did they use to call it, free love, was it, like that?'

I smiled, and told him love was never free. He'd learn, I said. But then I answered his question. Why not?

We had everything, I told him. Take a small community of healthy, active people trying to build a new way of life, then tell them to lose their inhibitions, tell them there aren't any rules and demonstrate by example. You're not going to get a rerun of the Victorians, are you? We had singles and couples, straights and gays;

more than one plural marriage, and more than one divorce. We were always shuffling people from house to house or bringing an old abandoned hut back into service, to accommodate a new grouping who wanted to be together or an established partnership who wanted to split.

Stephen was that rare thing, a singleton who really wanted to be alone. He built himself a hut on the fringes of the settlement, and never shared it in all the years the colony survived. Mostly, people thought he was doing it to prove a point that already didn't need proving, that he and his brother were poles apart.

There was always some question why Stephen was there at all; he made the settlement happen, but he never made himself a part of it. They murmured about him often, in groups over a communal fire or more privately in bed at night, and mostly they came up with the same answer again. If he hadn't been constantly there, constantly setting himself against Thomas for all to see the difference, people might have assumed that Thomas's brother was cast in the same mould as Thomas himself. Hard enough to live in that man's shadow, people said, worse still to be taken for his shadow. No, they said, Stephen stays because it's important to assert his independence, his separateness, and to do that he has to be here, where it can clearly be seen.

Or, less thoughtfully, they said, 'He's a bolshie little bugger, that Stephen. Place'd go to pot without him, but Christ he's hard sometimes. The way he sneers at Thomas, well, I wouldn't stand for it myself. You'd never know they were brothers, would you? I mean, would you?'

'Oh, yes,' someone else might say. 'Yes, I think they'd have to be. They couldn't be like that, else. I mean, Thomas just stands there and takes it, and I know he's a saint, but even so, I don't think even he would take that from anyone except a brother...'

If Stephen truly loved anyone in the settlement, it would have to be little Paul, his nephew. He used to walk the baby through the woods for hours, when he was colicky and wouldn't sleep; and later they would walk together, as far as Paul's stumpy legs would carry him. The boy would come back from these adventures riding on his uncle's shoulders, or else asleep in his arms; and would be full of tales afterwards of red squirrels and deer seen, of foxes' tracks and badgers visited who were too sleepy to come to the door of their setts when Stephen knocked. Paul was the one member of the community whom Stephen was always easy with, always patient; and the reverse was true too, or seemed to be, that if there was any one person that Paul loved more than equally, that person might be Stephen.

They ask me about fights and disputes in a society without rules, of course they do. Who adjudicated, they want to know, who was the policeman?

Sometimes I saw no one and there wasn't one, sometimes I say we all did, we all were. Both answers were true, but neither satisfies. So then I sidetrack, I take issue with their assumptions. Who says there weren't any rules? I ask. Of course there were rules, I tell them. It's only that they were so obvious, so taken for granted that they never needed writing down, they barely needed mentioning.

Everything was shared, everything was common, that was the primary rule. Whatever came in came to us, whatever went out went from us. We did everything together: we worked and played, raised a child, ate and talked and slept together. Put at its simplest, we lived all for one and one for all; or rather, we should have done. In practice, it never quite worked out that way.

In practice what we had, how we lived

was all for one and one for all, and Stephen.

Seven years the settlement lasted, all told. There was never any real trouble with the locals, and even the landowner was glad to have them there for the simple forestry and conservation work they did, logging fallen trees and keeping the stream clear, mending walls and watching for summer fires.

Seven years; and it ended in a single rainy night, when the wood was filled with screaming, and more than one life died too soon.

It had been building for a long time, of course, months or perhaps even years; and Stephen it was who built it, he was always the builder. Stephen it was who sat restless at the fire many nights that summer, digging his knife into the earth and glowering at Thomas through the flames, making strange demands.

'Tell them you're not a saint,' he said one time, with a contemptuous gesture at the listening disciples. 'Go on, tell them.'

'I'm not a saint,' Thomas said obligingly, smiling, *anything you want, Stephen. You're not heavy, you're my brother.*

'Now say it like you mean it. Go on, try. Try and believe it, why don't you?'

'I never say anything I don't mean,'

Thomas said, and meant it. 'Stephen, I don't understand. What's all this in aid of?'

'You're not leaving me any room,' in a vicious mutter, while his knife slashed and slashed. 'You're not leaving me any *choices*, Thomas.'

'I'm sorry, I don't understand that. You've got the same choices that any of us have.'

'No. No, that's not true. The rest of you don't have to live my life. Because if you're a saint, Thomas,' riding over the sighs and the strong denials, 'if you're a saint, then what the hell does that leave me? What does that *make* me?'

'Human, at a guess,' Thomas suggested, still smiling.

'I've tried that,' Stephen said, with a wild shake of the head. 'I've tried it, and it doesn't *work.*'

'Oh, come on, Stephen. Look around you. Of course it works, it's what we're best at. It's working pretty well here, isn't it? Wouldn't you say?'

'Oh, for you it works,' bitter and angry now. 'It works for *you*, that's what I'm saying. Doesn't work for me, though, does it? Does it?'

And Thomas looked at him, and for once didn't answer a question directly; because he wouldn't lie, he didn't know how to, and the truth was plain to see.

'You don't have to stay,' he said instead, gentle and understanding and unhappy. 'You can always leave, if you don't feel comfortable here. We'd be desperately sorry to lose you, you've given us so much, but...'

'I can't go,' Stephen said, with all his masks fallen away except perhaps one, except perhaps the last. 'I can't go, and leave all this behind me. I'm *invested* here. And you're not giving me any choice...'

And Stephen left the fire and walked away into the night, as he had done so often that summer. He left the company and the conversation brighter by his absence, even the firelight seemed brighter with him gone; but even so there were little shivers, there were goose-pimples to be rubbed down and lovers to be silently reassured. Because if Thomas was a saint—and no one doubted it except the man himself, his one blind spot, his failing—and Stephen was the opposite of his brother, if Stephen was working so hard to achieve that, then what *did* that make him? What was he working towards, where would it end?

Where it ended, of course, was that night of rain and screaming, and an unbridgeable gulf torn between brother and brother.

I make a point of telling new friends

about it. I tell them everything, except my true name; as far as that goes, Thomas Woodson will do, but I conceal nothing else. No one can share my burden, but I think it important that they at least understand where it came from.

Mostly they are quiet afterwards, caught awkwardly between sympathy and horror, nowhere that can be fitted easily into a package of words. After that, they're usually frightened to ask questions for a while; but they get there in the end, they're driven to it. That's when they ask about the others, and however do I manage on my own—and eventually, inevitably, someone will ask about Stephen, what happened to him.

And I tell them, I tell them even that. Why not? It's a pitiless world, let them learn.

It was a child's scream that split the wet night's noises, clean and tight as glass, and as fragile.

There was no communal fire that night, and seemingly no community; everyone was in their own house or hut, most in their own rooms, their own beds by now. It was early yet, but they lived a daylight life in any case, and the rain was a spoiler.

Even the ones who were sleeping heard the scream. And woke, and knew who made it even though they'd never heard it before, not like that. Even while they were talking of animals, a howling dog perhaps, they were sitting up and frantically scrabbling in darkness for their clothes.

Then he screamed again, and no talking now, they came tumbling from their houses into the rain. They ran to Thomas, and found him in the doorway of his house; and in his hand a note, a scrap of paper.

'This was on Paul's pillow,' he said. 'It's Stephen, he says, he says he's taken Paul to meet the badgers.'

Because it's not the sort of thing you'd think of, the note didn't say. *One last proof* it didn't say, it didn't need to.

Again Paul screamed, somewhere on the valley's slope, high above their heads; and this time there were words in it, but they were confused by distance and blurred by rain, and even his father could make no sense of them.

'Where are they?' Thomas demanded. 'Badgers, what does he mean, what's he *doing?*'

Silence, frantic looks and shrugs and shaking heads. Stephen was the one who knew about badgers, where the setts were and which were occupied. Others had seen holes in the ground, to be sure, and guessed their origin; but to find them again, in the dark, in the rain, in a panic?

'We'll just have to, have to follow the noise,' someone said. 'And call, let him know we're coming.'

'And pray he keeps screaming,' another voice. 'Sorry, Thomas, but it's the only way we'll find him.'

Everyone went to search. They shared this, as they shared it all; and not one would stay behind, not one was willing to be separated from their mutual terror.

'The more of us there are, the more ground we can cover,' they said. 'They're out there somewhere, we've just got to *find* them, that's what counts.'

So they started up the hill in a long file, taking sticks to help them on the muddy slopes; but they ended up finding another use for those, because Paul's screams did stop too soon. They were all but helpless then, in the dark and the rain and the fear, the confusion of it all. They used the sticks to beat the bushes, but it was frustration more than method; fury, almost seeking to thrash an answer out of the silent world.

And they shouted, they called Paul's name and Stephen's, and heard nothing but each other and their own muddled fancies, woven from hope and desperation mixed: 'Quiet, I thought I heard something then, will you be *quiet...*'

They found the badgers' sett at last,

and beside it a deep, steep-sided pit; but though Thomas jumped straight into it and felt with his hands in the muddy water collected at the bottom, he found nothing except deep furrows in the stony earth where it seemed an animal had scratched at it, or a child worked his fingers to the bone.

It was someone else who found Paul's clothes, kicked under a bush a few yards distant.

They searched on for an hour, for two hours, for three; and at last, sick and filthy and exhausted, one by one they turned back to the settlement again. Some were limping, some were in tears; the first to go were merely furtive, betraying their trust, sharing nothing any longer.

Someone took Paul's two mothers back eventually, dragged them almost, the last to give up, but Thomas stayed out. All night he stayed, walking and searching for as long as he had the strength, calling his son; and even when his legs and heart failed him, still he wouldn't go in. He dared not admit that his son was lost, for fear of making it true by his own acceptance; so he stood at the valley's heart, on the bridge that spanned the rising stream. He stood unmoving for hours, his big hands clenched around the rail and his head tipped back in the rain, straining for any sound that might be his son discovered.

And he heard nothing but the rain and the stream and the pebbles in the stream-bed rolling, until the morning came; and the first thing he heard in the morning was the sound of his own voice screaming.

His head had fallen by now, and his shoulders were bowed at last, though the rain had stopped; and his eyes could see something in the water below his feet, even before there was light enough to make out what it was.

Not even thinking by now, far too far gone to guess or wonder, he could only look at it until the light was better. Then he saw that there was a rope tied around the central upright, and a sack tied to the rope: a sack too large for its light contents, bobbing and tugging in the greedy water. Thomas stood staring for a long time, before he vaulted the rail and plunged waist-deep into the bitter stream.

Now he was urgent, now he didn't have time to fight the sodden, swollen knots and the rope was too short to reach the bank; so he lifted the sack onto the bridge, and drew himself up after. Sat on the worn wet planks and fumbled with the rope where it was tied around the sack's mouth, and still couldn't deal with the knots; so he took hold of the sack in two great handfuls, and heaved.

And even as the seam ripped apart, if he was thinking at all he must have been thinking *No*, thinking *It's too small, too light, if there's anything dead in here it'll be a badger, that's all. I don't know what game Stephen's playing but it's not that, at least it's not Paul...*

And even as the seam ripped, even as he thought his child safe—if he was thinking at all—he must have seen that he was wrong.

Badgers have savage teeth, and will fight viciously in a trap; but badger-bites were the least of what was done to Paul. That was just the start of it, when Stephen baited the badger with the boy for bait.

After that he used his knife. From the look of it in the weak morning sun, he'd done that work on the bridge, while the settlers searched the woods above. Even all the rain they'd had wasn't enough to hide new chips and gouges in the old wood, too darkly stained too soon.

And then Paul had gone in the sack and the sack had gone in the stream, tied where it could be neatly found in the morning; and the real sweet gift from Stephen to Thomas, brother to brother, was the knowledge that Paul might still have been alive when he went in the sack. Might still have been bleeding to death or slowly drowning, might still have been fighting for life while Thomas stood only a foot higher and a yard away, on the bridge in the deep dark of a cloudy country night.

I told them this story last week because they asked, they wanted to know what happened to end the settlement. It was right that they should know, and so I told them; and after the usual silence, the shifting around, the hunt for words that don't exist to express what cannot and should not be expressed, someone asked the question I'd been waiting for.

'Thomas, and what...what happened to Stephen?'

'Nothing,' I said. 'Nothing happened to Stephen. He'd proved his point and gone, and that was all. He disappeared.'

'But surely, the police, surely they could find him...'

I shook my head. 'No police. They were never told. The colony must have been scattered long before they even heard rumours, and no one left a forwarding address. So they had no witnesses, no body, even the bridge was gone by then, no evidence there—nothing they could do, really, except file and forget. Journalists the same. They still catch hints of it, they ask questions; but I won't talk to journalists and they don't know where else to turn. No handle, no story. File and forget.'

That was about the last communal decision they made: that even in desolation, even in their final days they had to cling to the dream. The evil was theirs to be shared among them, and the outer world had no claim. So they dealt with Paul's body in their own way, and then they left. Not together, they could never do anything together any more; but in ones and twos they went, walking or hitching or catching a bus, barely saying goodbye and leaving almost everything behind them.

In a week the settlement was empty, but for Thomas. He stayed a few days on his own, one wife gone south and the other west, talking of America; then he too was gone one morning, the bridge burned behind him and he never came back.

That's the story as I tell it, as I told it to my art class. Privileged information, I told them, keep it to yourselves. And they did, I think, generally they do. It's too terrible for common gossip.

But last night I was drinking on the Quayside a few minutes' walk from my flat, when one of my pupils came in with a much older woman.

Ailie saw me, and waved, and brought her companion over.

'Thomas,' she said, 'meet my friend Kate. Kate, this is Thomas, he teaches that art class I go to...'

But, 'Oh, no,' Kate said, staring at me, twenty years unmasked on her face. 'No,' she said, 'oh, no. That isn't Thomas,' she said, 'that's Stephen.'

I should be teaching my class tonight, but I don't think I'll go. If I did go, I don't think there would be anybody there.

I believe my brother is dead. I think he must be; I cannot see how he could have lived this long, or why he would have wanted to, or where he would have gone.

So I live his life for him, as best I can. This is the final irony, if you like: that having shown myself so different, having given so much to prove it, I must now come as close as I am able. I am not a saint, of course, but I wear his name, and try to keep on the side of the angels now. They were right not to pursue me, with their own justice or other people's. It would have been quite wasted.

I am Thomas for a few months here and a few months there, as long as I can bear it in any one place. I make friends, I work, and I tell his story. They deserve that much from me, he and Paul both.

I don't know what they did with Paul. I wasn't there to see. Perhaps they buried him in the pit beside the badgers, it would have been convenient; perhaps elsewhere in the wood. Perhaps they fed him to the badgers, I don't know.

I loved that boy. I had to, or I couldn't have done what I did. It wouldn't have been right, done without love.

I wish I knew where he was buried, I'd like to visit him; but having once got away, I cannot go back to the wood.

I live with bridges always in my view, inescapable as water; but I cannot bear, I cannot *bear* to walk across a bridge.

3

A Winter's Tale
by
ANN CLEEVES

In the hills there had been snow for five days, the first real snow of the winter. In town it had turned to rain, bitter and unrelenting, and in Otterbridge it had seemed dark all day. As Ramsay drove out of the coastal plain and began the climb up Cheviot the clouds broke and there was a shaft of sunshine which reflected blindingly on the snow. For days he had been depressed by the weather and the gaudy festivities of the season, but as the cloud lifted he felt suddenly more optimistic.

Hunter, sitting hunched beside him, remained gloomy. It was the Saturday before Christmas and he had better things to do. He always left his shopping until the last minute—he enjoyed being part of the crowds in Newcastle. Christmas meant getting pissed in the heaving pubs on the Bigg Market, sharing drinks with tipsy secretaries who seemed to spend the last week of work in a continuous office party. It meant wandering up Northumberland Street where children queued to peer in at the magic of Fenwick's window and listening to the Sally Army band playing carols at the entrance to Eldon Square. It had nothing to do with all this space and the bloody cold. Like a Roman stationed on Hadrian's Wall, Hunter thought the wilderness was barbaric.

Ramsay said nothing. The road had been cleared of snow but was slippery and driving took concentration. Hunter was itching to get at the wheel—he had been invited to a party in a club in Blyth and it took him as long as a teenage girl to get ready for a special evening out.

Ramsay turned carefully off the road, across a cattle grid and onto a track.

'Bloody hell!' Hunter said. 'Are we going to get up here?'

'The farmer said it was passable. He's been down with a tractor.'

'I'd better get the map,' Hunter said miserably. 'I suppose we've got a grid reference. I don't fancy getting lost out there.'

'I don't think that'll be necessary,' Ramsay said. 'I've been to the house before.'

Hunter did not ask about Ramsay's previous visit to Blackstoneburn. The

69

Inspector rarely volunteered information about his social life or friends. And apart from an occasional salacious curiosity about Ramsay's troubled marriage and divorce Hunter did not care. Nothing about the Inspector would have surprised him.

The track no longer climbed but crossed a high and empty moor. The horizon was broken by a dry stone wall and a derelict barn but otherwise there was no sign of habitation. Hunter felt increasingly uneasy. Six geese flew from a small reservoir to circle overhead and settle back once the car had passed.

'Greylags,' Ramsay said. 'Wouldn't you say?'

'I don't bloody know.' Hunter had not been able to identify them even as geese. And I don't bloody care, he thought.

The sun was low in the sky ahead of them. Soon it would be dark. They must have driven over an imperceptible ridge because suddenly, caught in the orange sunlight, there was a house, grey, small-windowed, a fortress of a place surrounded by byres and outhouses.

'That's it, is it?' Hunter said, relieved. It hadn't, after all, taken so long. The party wouldn't warm up until the pubs shut. He would make it in time.

'No,' Ramsay said. 'That's the farm. It's another couple of miles yet.'

He was surprised by the pleasure he took in Hunter's discomfort, and a little ashamed. He thought his relationship with his sergeant was improving. Yet it wouldn't do Hunter any harm, he thought, to feel anxious and out of place. On his home ground he was intolerably confident.

The track dipped to a ford. The path through the water was rocky and the burn was frozen at the edges. Ramsay accelerated carefully up the bank and as the back wheels spun he remembered his previous visit to Blackstoneburn. It had been high summer, the moor scorched with drought, the burn dried up almost to a trickle. He had thought he would never come to the house again.

As they climbed away from the ford they saw the Black Stone, surrounded by open moor. It was eight feet high, truly black with the setting sun behind it, throwing a shadow onto the snow.

Hunter stared and whistled under his breath but said nothing. He would not give his boss the satisfaction of asking for information. The information came anyway. Hunter thought Ramsay could have been one of those guides in bobble hats and walking boots who worked at weekends for the National Park.

'It's part of a circle of prehistoric stones,' the Inspector said. 'Even if there weren't any snow you wouldn't see the others at this distance. The bracken's grown over them.' He seemed lost for a moment in memory. 'The house was named after the stone of course. There's been a dwelling on this site since the fourteenth century.'

'A bloody daft place to put a house,' Hunter muttered. 'If you ask me...'

They looked down into a valley onto an L-shaped house, built around a flagged yard, surrounded by windblown trees and shrubs.

'According to the farmer,' Ramsay said, 'the dead woman wasn't one of the owner's family...'

'So what the hell was she doing here?' Hunter demanded. The emptiness made him belligerent. 'It's not the sort of place you'd stumble on by chance.'

'It's a holiday cottage,' Ramsay said. 'Of sorts. Owned by a family from Otterbridge called Shaftoe. They don't let it out commercially but friends know that they can stay here... The strange thing is that the farmer said there was no car...'

The track continued up the hill and had, Hunter supposed, some obscure agricultural use. Ramsay turned off it down a pot-holed drive and stopped in the yard, which because of the way the wind had been blowing was almost clear of snow. A dirty green Land Rover was already parked there and as they approached a tall, bearded man got out and stood impassively, waiting for them to emerge from the warmth of their car. The sun had disappeared and the air was icy.

'Mr Helms.' The Inspector held out his hand. 'I'm Ramsay. Northumbria Police.'

'Aye,' the man said. 'Well, I'd not have expected it to be anyone else.'

'Can we go in?' Hunter demanded. 'It's freezing out here.'

Without a word the farmer led them to the front of the house. The wall was half-covered with ivy and already the leaves were beginning to be tinged with frost. The front door led directly into a living room. In a grate the remains of a fire smouldered but there was little warmth. The three men stood awkwardly just inside the room.

'Where is she?' Hunter asked.

'In the kitchen,' the farmer said. 'Out the back.'

Hunter stamped his feet impatiently, expecting Ramsay to lead the way. He knew the house. But Ramsay stood, looking around him.

'Had Mr Shaftoe asked you to keep an eye on the place?' he asked. 'Or did something attract your attention?'

'There was someone here last night,' Helms said. 'I saw a light from the back.'

'Was there a car?'

73

'Don't know. Didn't notice.'

'By man, you're a lot of help,' Hunter muttered. Helms pretended not to hear.

'But you might have noticed,' Ramsay persisted, 'fresh tyre tracks on the drive.'

'Look,' Helms said, 'Shaftoe lets me use one of his barns. I'm up and down the track every day. If someone had driven down using my tracks how would I know?'

'Were you surprised to see a light?' Ramsay asked.

'Not really,' Helms said. 'They don't have to tell me when they're coming up.'

'Could they have made it up the track from the road?'

'Shaftoe could. He's got one of those posh Japanese four-wheel-drive jobs.'

'Is it usual for him to come up in the Winter?'

'Aye.' Helms was faintly contemptuous. 'They have a big do on Christmas Eve. I'd thought maybe they'd come up to air the house for that. No-one's been in the place for months.'

'You didn't hear a vehicle go back down the track last night?'

'No. But I wouldn't have done. The father-in-law's stopping with us and he's deaf as a post. He has the telly so loud you can't hear a thing.'

'What time did you see the light?'

Helms shrugged. 'Seven o'clock maybe.

74

I didn't go out after that.'

'But you didn't expect them to be staying?'

'No. Like I said. I expected them to light a fire, check the calor gas, clean up a bit and then go back.'

'So what caught your attention this morning?'

'The gas light was still on,' Helms said.

'In the same room?'

Helms nodded. 'The kitchen. It was early, still pretty dark outside and I thought they must have stayed and were getting their breakfasts. It was only later when the kids got me to bring them over, that I thought it was strange.'

'I don't understand,' Ramsay said. 'Why did your children want to come?'

'Because they're sharp little buggers. It's just before Christmas. They thought Shaftoe would have a present for them. He usually brings them something, Christmas or not.'

'So you drove them down in the Land Rover? What time was that?'

'Just before dinner. Twelvish. They'd been out sledging and Chrissie my wife said there was more snow on her kitchen floor than out on the fell. I thought I'd earn a few brownie points by getting them out of her hair.' He paused and for the first time he smiled. 'I thought I'd get a drink for my trouble. Shaftoe always kept a supply of malt whisky in the place and he was never mean with it.'

'Did you park in the yard?'

'Aye. Like I always do.'

'That's when you noticed the light was still on?'

Helms nodded.

'What did you do then?'

'Walked round here to the front.'

'Had it been snowing?' Ramsay asked.

'There were a couple of inches in the night but it was clear by dawn.'

'What about footprints on the path? You would have noticed if the snow had been disturbed.'

'Aye,' Helms said. 'I might have done if I'd got the chance. But I let the dog and the bairns out of the Land Rover first and they chased round to the front before me.'

'But your children might have noticed,' Ramsay insisted.

'Aye,' Helms said without much hope. 'They might.'

'Did they go into the house before you?'

'No. They were still on the front lawn throwing snowballs about when I joined them. That's when I saw the door was open and I started to think something was up. I told the kids to wait outside and came in on my own. I stood in here feeling a bit daft and shouted out the back to Shaftoe. When there was no reply I went on through.'

'What state was the fire in?' Ramsay asked.

'Not much different from what it's like now. If you bank it up it stays like that for hours.'

There was a pause. 'Come on then,' Ramsay said. 'We'd best go through and look at her.'

The kitchen was lit by two gas lamps mounted on one wall. The room was small and functional. There was a small window covered on the outside by bacterial-shaped whirls of ice, a stainless steel sink and a row of units. The woman, lying with one cheek against the red tiles, took up most of the available floor space. Ramsay, looking down, recognised her immediately.

'Joyce,' he said. 'Rebecca Joyce.' He looked at Helms. 'She was a friend of the Shaftoe family. You don't recognise her?'

The farmer shook his head.

Ramsay had met Rebecca Joyce at Blackstoneburn. Diana had invited him to the house when their marriage was in its final throes and he had gone out of desperation thinking that on her own ground, surrounded by her family and friends, she might be calmer. Diana was related to the Shaftoes by marriage. Her younger sister Isobel had married one of the Shaftoe sons and at that summer house-party they were all there: old man Shaftoe who had made his money out of scrap, Isobel and her husband Stuart, a grey, thin-lipped man who had brought the family respectability by proposing to the daughter of one of the most established landowners in Northumberland.

Rebecca had been invited as a friend, solely it seemed to provide entertainment. She had been at school with Diana and Isobel and had been outrageous apparently even then. Looking down at the body on the cold kitchen floor, Ramsay thought that despite the battered skull he still saw a trace of the old spirit.

'I'll be off then...' Helms interrupted his daydream. 'If there's nothing else.'

'No,' Ramsay said. 'I'll know where to find you.'

'Aye. Well.' He sloped off, relieved. They heard the Land Rover drive away up the track and then it was very quiet.

'The murder weapon was a poker,' Hunter said. 'Hardly original.'

'Effective though.' It still lay on the kitchen floor, the ornate brass knob covered with blood.

'What now?' Hunter demanded. Time

was moving on. It was already six o'clock. In another hour his friends would be gathering in the pubs of Otterbridge preparing for the party.

'Nothing,' Ramsay said, 'until the pathologist and the scene-of-crime team arrive.' He knew that Hunter wanted to be away. He could have sent him off in the car, arranged a lift for himself with the colleagues who would arrive later, earned for a while some gratitude and peace, but a perverseness kept him quiet and they sat in the freezing living room, waiting.

When Ramsay met Rebecca Joyce it had been hot, astoundingly hot for the Northumberland hills, and they had taken their drinks outside onto the lawn. Someone had slung a hammock between two Scotch Pines and Diana had lain there moodily, not speaking, refusing to acknowledge his presence. They had rowed in the car on the way to Blackstoneburn and he was forced to introduce himself to Tom Shaftoe, a small squat man with silver sideburns. Priggish Isobel and anonymous Stuart he had met before. The row had been his fault. Diana had not come home the night before and he had asked quietly, restraining his jealousy, where she had been. She had lashed out in a fury, condemning him for his Methodist morals, his dullness.

'You're just like your mother,' she had said. The final insult. 'All hypocrisy and thrift.' Then she had fallen stubbornly and guiltily silent and had said nothing more to him all evening.

Was it because of her taunts that he had gone with Rebecca to look at the Black Stone? Rebecca wore a red lycra tube which left her shoulders bare and scarcely covered her buttocks. She had glossy red lipstick and black curls pinned back with combs. She had been flirting shamelessly with Stuart all evening and then suddenly to Ramsay she said:

'Have you ever seen the stone circle?'

He shook his head, surprised, confused by her sudden interest.

'Come on then,' she had said. 'I'll show you.'

In the freezing room at Blackstoneburn Hunter looked at his boss and thought he was a mean bastard, a killjoy. There was no need for them both to be there. He nodded towards the kitchen door, bored by the silence, irritated because Ramsay would not share information about the dead woman.

'What did she do then?' he asked. 'For a living.'

Ramsay took a long time to reply and Hunter wondered if he were ill, if he was losing his grip completely.

'She would say,' the Inspector answered at last, 'that she lived off her wits.'

He had assumed, because she had been to school with Diana and Isobel, that her family were wealthy, but discovered later that her father had been a hopeless and irresponsible businessman. A wild scheme to develop a Roman theme park on some land close to Hadrian's Wall had led to bankruptcy and Rebecca had left school early because the fees could not be paid. It was said that the teachers were glad of an excuse to be rid of her.

'By man,' said Hunter. 'What does that mean?'

'She had a few jobs,' Ramsay said. 'She managed a small hotel for a while, ran the office of the agricultural supply place in Otterbridge. But she couldn't stick any of them. I suppose it means she lived off men.'

'She was a whore?'

'I suppose,' Ramsay said, 'it was something like that.'

'You seem to know a lot about her. Did you know her well, like?'

The insolence was intended. Ramsay ignored it.

'No,' he said. 'I only met her once.'

But I was interested, he thought, interested enough to find out more about her, attracted not so much by the body in

81

the red lycra dress, but by her kindness. It was the show, the decadent image which put me off. If I had been braver I would have ignored it.

Her attempt to seduce him on that hot summer night had been a kindness, an offer of comfort. Away from the house she had taken his hand and they had crossed the burn by stepping stones, like children. She had shown him the round black stones hidden by bracken and then put his hand on her round, lycra-covered breast.

He had hesitated, held back by his Methodist morals and the thought of sad Diana lying in the hammock on the lawn. Rebecca had been kind again, unoffended.

'Don't worry,' she said, laughing, kissing him lightly on the cheek. 'Not now. If you need me you'll be able to find out where I am.'

And she had run away back to the others, leaving him to follow slowly, giving him time to compose himself.

Ramsay was so engrossed in the memory of his encounter with Rebecca Joyce that he did not hear the vehicles outside or the sound of voices. He was jolted back to the present by Hunter shouting: 'There they are. About bloody time too.' And by the scene-of-crime team at the door bending to change their shoes, complaining cheerfully about the cold.

'Right then,' Hunter said. 'We can leave it to the reinforcements.' He looked at his watch. Seven o'clock. The timing would be tight but not impossible. 'I suppose someone should see the Shaftoes tonight,' he said. 'They're the most likely suspects. I'd volunteer for the overtime myself but I'm all tied up this evening.'

'I'll talk to the Shaftoes,' Ramsay said. It was the least he could do.

Outside in the dark it was colder than ever. Ramsay's car would not start immediately and Hunter swore under his breath. At last it pulled away slowly, the heater began to work and he began to relax.

'I want to call at the farm,' Ramsay said. 'Just to clear up a few things.'

'Bloody hell!' Hunter said, convinced that Ramsay was prolonging the journey just to spite him. 'What's the matter now?'

'This is a murder enquiry,' Ramsay said sharply. 'Not just an interruption to your social life.'

'You'll not get anything from that Helms,' Hunter said. 'What could he know, living up here? It's enough to drive anyone crazy.'

Ramsay said nothing. He thought that Helms was unhappy, not mad.

'Rebecca always goes for lonely men,'

Diana had said cruelly on the drive back from Blackstoneburn that summer. 'It's the only way she can justify screwing around.'

'What's your justification?' he could have said, but Diana was unhappy too and there had seemed little point.

They parked in the farm yard. In a shed cattle moved and made gentle noises. A small woman with fine pale hair tied back in an untidy pony-tail let them into the kitchen where Helms was sitting in a high-backed chair, his stockinged feet stretched ahead of him. He was not surprised to see them. The room was warm despite the stone flag floor. A clothes horse, held together with binder twine, was propped in front of the range and children's jeans and jerseys steamed gently. The uncurtained window was misted with condensation. Against one wall was a large square table covered by a patterned oil cloth, with a pile of drawing books and a scattering of felt-tipped pens. From another room came the sound of a television and the occasional shriek of a small child.

Chrissie Helms sat by the table. She had big hands, red and chapped, which she clasped around her knees.

'I need to know,' Ramsay said gently, 'exactly what happened.'

Hunter looked at the fat clock ticking

on the mantelpiece and thought his boss was mad.

Ramsay turned to the farmer. 'You were lying,' he said. 'It's so far-fetched, you see. Contrived. A strange and beautiful woman found miles from anywhere in the snow. Like a film. It must be simpler than that. You would have seen tracks when you took the tractor up to the road to clear a path for us. It's lonely out here. If you'd seen a light in Blackstoneburn last night you'd have gone in. Glad of the company and old Shaftoe's whisky.'

Helms shook his head helplessly.

'Did he pay you to keep quiet?' Hunter demanded. Suddenly, with a reluctant witness to bully he was in his element. 'Or did he threaten you?'

'No,' Helms said, 'it were nothing like that.'

'But she was there with some man?' Hunter was jubilant.

'Oh,' Helms' wife said quietly, shocking them with her interruption. 'She was there with some man.'

Ramsay turned to the farmer. 'She was your mistress?' he said, and Hunter realised he had known all along.

Helms said nothing.

'You must have met her at the agricultural suppliers in Otterbridge. Perhaps when you went to pay your bill. Perhaps

85

she recognised you. She often came to Blackstoneburn.'

'I recognised her,' Helms said.

'You'd hardly miss her,' the woman said. 'The way she flaunted herself.'

'No,' the farmer shook his head. 'No, it wasn't like that.'

He paused.

'You felt sorry for her...?' Ramsay prompted.

'Aye!' Helms looked up, relieved to be understood at last.

'Why did you bring her here?' Ramsay asked.

'I didn't. Not here.'

'But to Blackstoneburn. You had a key? Or Rebecca did?'

Helms nodded. 'She was lonely,' he said. 'In town. Everyone thinking of Christmas. You know.'

'So you brought her up to Blackstoneburn,' Hunter said unpleasantly. 'For a dirty weekend. Thinking you'd sneak over to spend some time with her. Thinking your wife wouldn't notice.'

Helms said nothing.

'What went wrong?' Hunter demanded. 'Did she get greedy? Want more money? Blackmail? Is that why you killed her?'

'You fool!' It was almost a scream and as she spoke the woman stood up with her huge red hands laid flat on the table. 'He wouldn't have harmed her. He didn't kill her. I did.'

'You must tell me,' Ramsay said again, 'exactly what happened.'

But she needed no prompting. She was desperate for their understanding. 'You don't know what it's like here,' she said. 'Especially in the winter. Dark all day. Every year it drives me mad...' She stopped, realising she was making little sense and continued more rationally. 'I knew he had a woman, guessed. Then I saw them in town and I recognised her too. She was wearing black stockings and high heels, a dress that cost a fortune. How could I compare with that?' She looked down at her shapeless jersey and jumble sale trousers. 'I thought he'd grow out of it, if I ignored it, he'd stop. I never thought he'd bring her here.' She paused.

'How did you find out?' Ramsay asked.

'Yesterday afternoon I went out for a walk. I left the boys with my dad. I'd been in the house all day and just needed to get away from them all. It was half past three, starting to get dark. I saw the light in Blackstoneburn and Joe's Land Rover parked outside. Like you said we're desperate here for company so I went round to the front and knocked at the door. I thought Tom Shaftoe was giving him a drink.'

'There was no car,' Ramsay said.

'No,' she said. 'But Tom parks it sometimes in one of the sheds. I didn't suspect a thing.'

'Did you go in?'

'Not then,' she said calmly. 'When there was no reply I looked through the window. They were lying together in front of the fire. Then I went in...' She paused again. 'When she saw me she got up and straightened her clothes. She laughed. I suppose she was embarrassed. She said it was an awkward situation and why didn't we all discuss it over a cup of tea. Then she turned her back on me and walked through to the kitchen.' Chrissie Helms caught her breath in a sob. 'She shouldn't have turned her back,' she said. 'I deserved more than that...'

'So you hit her,' Ramsay said.

'I lost control,' Chrissie said. 'I picked up the poker from the grate and I hit her.'

'Did you mean to kill her?'

'I wasn't thinking clearly enough to mean anything.'

'But you didn't stop to help her?'

'No,' she said. 'I came home. I left it to Joe to sort out. He owed me that. He did his best but I knew we'd not be able to carry it through.' She looked at her husband. 'I'll miss you and the boys,' she said. 'But I'll not miss this place. Prison'll not be much different from this.'

Hunter walked to the window to wait for the police Land Rover. He rubbed a space in the condensation and saw that it was snowing again, heavily. He thought that he agreed with her.

4

The Good Old Days
by
EILEEN DEWHURST

When I was a child in my father's car I used to count the pubs on the corners of the long straight street leading out of Liverpool to my grandmother's. I only looked to my left but I never managed to keep up, the blocks of small shops were broken so regularly by side roads of back-to-back houses, every break angled on a pub.

It's a long time since I've travelled that way, and I wouldn't be travelling it this sunny August morning if they hadn't found a skeleton under the floor of the shed behind the flats where thirty years ago my grandmother lived. My grandmother's dead and I live across the Mersey in Wirral, but when I heard where the skeleton had been hiding I shouted out loud. After I'd explained my behaviour my Chief in Birkenhead CID requested his opposite number to give me a special place on the inquiry.

The Liverpool Chief asked me what I remembered, and when I said I remembered the sheds being built he suggested I call on the only inhabitant of the flats who was living there those years ago—his team has got that far without me—in the hope we'll be able to jog one another's memories.

At the same time he indicated that Mr Tomlinson is doing quite well on his own. 'You don't remember anything particular happening round the time of the building, then, Inspector Jenkins?'

'No, sir.'

'Mr Tomlinson appears to. I'll leave it to him to remind you.'

But he's filled me in, of course, on the modern situation. The skeleton's female, said by forensics to have been in her thirties when she met her death. No clues in her bones as to how that came about, and we'll be lucky if the teeth are any help after so long, seeing that she could be any woman missing in Liverpool at the time of her death, disappearance reported or not. At least we know she's been dead for three decades: the Council has come up with a copy of its approval in writing for the shed to be built, and till last week it hadn't been touched.

If I'd wanted to count pubs on my journey this morning I'd have found it easier. The ones that are still there are standing now in isolation beside sprawls of bulldozed bricks, or brave new unadorned constructions that make them look like fadedly bedizened dwarfs. I'd like to believe they've been rescued by the conservationists, but I know they're just temporarily reprieved to mark the spot a brewery must mark physically if it wants to retain its licence through the blitz of reconstruction.

Most of those side streets to the left have vanished with the destruction of their terrace patterns, and to my right I can see two vast tower blocks rising out of featureless balding grass.

It's absurd to feel so shaken, a slum's a slum however cosy the memories it calls up. And at least there's a chance the blocks of flats may follow the terraced houses into dust, we've learned now that they aren't indestructible. The grubby old church has gone, too, but I remember reading about a fire. The replacement has a roof of frosted glass panels arranged in waves.

Fine weather makes a street like this even more depressing than cloud and rain. When it was intact it was dreary and now it's terrible, dust swirling in the sun shafts and no green in sight until I turn up the Avenue. It's a relief to find that the tall trees still divide it, although I was hopeful they'd be there, seeing that the area has been listed as one of the earliest and best council developments in England. But the tram-tracks along the centre have gone, of course. There's just a sandy path where they used to be. If anyone offered me a sound from my childhood I'd choose the trams pulling up the Avenue as I heard them at night when I lay in bed.

I thought the Avenue might have shrunk because of being so grand in my child's memory, but it's still a fine wide road, lined both sides with twenties- and thirties-built flats. My grandmother's section, a bit later than the neo-classic, completed the Avenue's development in Tudor style, with "own front doors" opening on to the outside instead of a communal interior—a big plus at the time of first letting. The ground floor flats give on to short but artistically winding concrete paths bisecting small neat lawns (Council gardeners take care of them), and those on the first and second floors have front doors at right angles on the same level—the top people do their final climb in private—up a flight of concrete steps. The steps were tricky for an elderly lady to negotiate, and within a week of buying them my grandmother lost most of the leather off the backs of a new pair of shoes. The flight still feels steep.

As I climb I have a glimpse of green through the entry below. When the flats were built each tenant was given a small fenced oblong of garden in the house-fringed triangle of land at the back, the far side of the concrete path where I used to cycle up and down. I can see now what triumphs they were of even-handed compression. They must have been moved about a lot on paper before the planners got them to fit together with the minimum omission of ground. I can't remember how we got into my grandmother's without setting foot on someone else's exclusive territory, I just know that we did, and I'll never find out because the gardens and the fences have gone.

It was a recent Council decision, urged by the current residents, to pull down the fences and make one shapely garden for all, that brought the skeleton to light: the brick shed, the only communal component of the old garden scheme, stood literally in the way of the new.

The Liverpool Chief has filled me in on the whys and wherefores that hadn't concerned me as a child: the residents decided at one of their meetings to ask the Council if between them they could build a shed and divide it inside to take their strictly individual garden tools. They'd like it in brick, they said, with a cement floor, but they didn't specify a skeleton to go underneath it.

The Council agreed, and gave them the largest chunk of the land that had refused to fit into their scheme of private rectangles—the centre point of the triangle furthest from the flats, behind the only clump of trees on the site. The back ones had to be cut down to make room for the shed, but conservation wasn't so much of an issue, then. I remember being enthusiastic for a few days about helping (or hindering) whoever was working on the shed—passing up bricks and so on—before getting bored with the enterprise and going back to my bicycle.

My temporary Chief asked me, unhope-fully, if I remembered who worked on the floor, and to my surprise I got a picture—of a man in the twilight humping a sack through the open door. Wishful thinking, perhaps, but the man doesn't have a face or a height so it isn't important whether or not the picture's an original. I have a feeling, though, that it's incomplete, and the Chief told me to keep on working at it.

And visit Mr Tomlinson.

Mr Tomlinson left the Avenue a long time before my grandmother died, his wife came from Scotland and they went to live up there. I can remember drinking lemonade at their farewell party and watching some of the grown-ups get excited and rosy-faced. Then I remember waving them off, I can see Mrs Tomlinson's bright hair through the passenger window of their car, but I don't suppose they went immediately the party was over. The Chief told me Mr Tomlinson had been in insurance in Liverpool, and made a successful request for a transfer. I hadn't remembered that, but even if I'd heard it at the time it wouldn't have been the sort of information I'd take in.

The Chief also told me that Mrs Tomlinson died a few years ago, and that her Liverpudlian husband decided then that he'd like to come home. He'll tell me about that, too.

Amazingly Mr Tomlinson got his old flat back, exactly opposite my grandmother's, so I've just climbed the same set of steps I climbed so often as a child. They're still half smothered in goldenrod, which I remember as always in flower. It's in flower now and I feel sentimentally nostalgic, but I'm encouraging it, that way memory may lie.

The knocker feels familiar in my hand, and the sound of it is almost as evocative as the trams. While I'm wondering if I remember Mr Tomlinson he appears at his shiny black front door, and I discover in the same instant that I do, and that he's changed. Smaller, thinner, abundant brown hair now abundant grey, but still with a lively blue eye, and the same potentially mocking smile. I'm recalling with a slight sense of shock that as a child I was scared of Mr Tomlinson, suspecting he could see through me.

'Ah! Detective Inspector Jenkins! I can't say I'd have known you, Billy.' Mr Tomlinson stands aside, gesturing me into the flat, and I graze past him into the narrow hall, the mirror image of my grandmother's, hearing the familiar forgotten sound of the front door closing as I look round, the nostalgia swelling. 'But forgive me, Inspector, perhaps it's Bill now, or even William?' He leads the way into the sitting-room.

'It's Billy to the people who called me Billy. How are you, Mr Tomlinson?'

'Can't grumble. This business has upset me, though. Nasty. Especially as I always rather liked Jim Mallory. Mustn't rush to conclusions, though...'

Jim Mallory. The schoolmaster above my grandmother with the surprisingly glamorous wife. Forgotten images rising in sharp focus from my memory bed.

'Billy has trouble with his Maths, Mr Mallory.' The schoolmaster almost falling over my grandmother and me as he charged down the concrete steps past the goldenrod.

'Oh, dear.' The schoolmaster grinding to a halt, breathing heavily as if his engine was continuing to run. Mr Mallory was always in a hurry, a state which I realise now must have warred with his kindly instincts to be of help to everyone. He leaned down from his skinny height, his untidy hair flopping on his forehead, his spectacles very large, to peer at me compassionately. 'Yes, I'm afraid it can be a difficult subject.' He must have turned then to my grandmother. 'I wouldn't want to interfere with his teachers, but if there's ever a specific problem...'

There never was, at least not acute enough for me to take Jim Mallory up on his kind offer. Or, more accurately, voluntarily to surrender an hour or two of freedom. But I was still quite happy to bump into our schoolmaster, confident he wouldn't say anything again about helping me with my Maths if I didn't, even when his wife invited me in for a chocolate and a chat. But that was usually when he was at school. Mrs Mallory was fair, and the aura of beauty and glamour around her is still so dazzling I've no real memory of what she looked like...

'Jim Mallory? I liked him, too.'
'Everyone did. Coffee, Bill? It's ready.'

'Thanks, Mr Tomlinson. Why did you say—'

'You might call me Fred, if you don't find it too difficult. If you do, I'll still answer to Mr Tomlinson.'

'Thanks,' I mumble as he leaves the room. I'm chagrined to find he still has his old effect on me, but while he's in the kitchen I'm having a policeman's look round. Purely from habit, if he'd had anything to do with the skeleton he'd hardly be proclaiming it via the decor of his sitting-room. I remember it dark and over-furnished, a time capsule like my grandmother's, but now it's painted white and the furniture is sparse and modern. Can't be the influence of his wife, even as a child I was aware of her strength of character; Mrs Tomlinson had to have been the setter of the domestic scene so she had to have liked dark brown paint and a lot of heavy furniture...

'Billy! Billy Jenkins!'

'Yes, Mrs Tomlinson?'

'Have you nothing to do but swing on those railings?' Scottish accent strong. Perhaps that's why I'm always prepared to be in awe of the Scots character.

'I'm waiting for my friend, Mrs Tomlinson, I've a friend coming to stay.' There were no children living in the flats and

99

it could get lonely, but my grandmother encouraged young visitors.

'Hm. When are your mother and father coming home?'

'I don't know.' I loved my grandmother, but a tear pricked behind my eye. I remember not wanting Mrs Tomlinson to see it, although I knew she wasn't really unkind.

'I expect it won't be long.' Her hair used to glint in the light. It was bright yellow, too fair for her rather red face, but she was big and handsome. It could have been then or some other time that she gave me a sweet.

'I was sorry to hear about your wife, Fred.'

Fred Tomlinson is putting the tray down on a fibreglass table.

'Yes. I miss her. She had cancer. Milk? Sugar?'

'A dash of milk. No sugar. Thanks. I remember her. I remember you both. Now. I didn't before you opened your front door.'

'That's how it goes.' His eyes are twinkling at me keenly. 'That's what the Chief Superintendent was hoping.'

But for the moment I'm caught up in my personal curiosity. 'What made you come back here? And how on earth did you get the same flat again?'

'Strange, wasn't it? I felt it was a sign I was doing the right thing.' Mr Tomlinson gets to his feet with a slight struggle, and carries his coffee to the bay window—when I was very small I used to crouch on my grandmother's wide sill—where he stands gazing out at the trees. 'I was happy enough in Scotland while I had Eunice, but when she died I felt like an exile. I'm a through and through Liverpudlian, Billy. But I'd lived in these flats for so many years before we left that I didn't know where to start. So I went to the Council and they told me my old flat was empty. They were on the point of offering it, but there was another free up the road and they said they could offer that instead, if I'd like this one back. Even Councils, it appears, sometimes have hearts. I said yes, of course, thinking I could always move.'

'And will you?'

He comes slowly away from the window, sits down again, and smiles at me. 'I don't suppose so.'

'Your flat used to be like my grand-mother's. It's different now.'

He laughs. 'We'd inherited most of the heavy stuff, we took the opportunity to get rid of it. I didn't bring much back with me, you don't feel the same need of possessions as you get older.'

'It must have felt strange, with no one else left.'

'I'm self-sufficient, Billy, if I can't have my wife I'm happy enough on my own. I still take photographs.'

'I'd forgotten!' And there are none in this anonymous room to remind me. 'You took that one of my grandmother!'

'I did take one of her. Is she still with you?'

'She died twenty years ago. My parents are alive. Near Nantwich.'

'So your father retired from the tobacco trade. You used to miss them, didn't you? It always took you a while to perk up when you first came to the flats.'

I laugh, although his words strike a bit of a painful note as I remember how when my parents took their trips to South America I wasn't always as grateful as I could have been for my beloved grandmother. 'You noticed.'

'Eunice did. She was sorry for you.' I realise with another little shock that she had shown it. 'And you, Billy?'

'Married with a son and a daughter. Living over the water, as my grandmother used to call the Wirral. Maybe that's why when I was small I thought the Mersey was the only waterway in the world, and that everyone and everything was one side of it or the other...'

Mr Tomlinson's amused, but it's time I was at work rather than down memory lane. It's just that so many are crowding to the surface they're making me feel punchdrunk. And more and more aware that one of them at least is missing.

'The Council has supplied a list of all the tenants at the time of the shed-building, but apart from the ones in our two blocks they're hardly more than names to me, I suppose because they didn't have children.'

Mr Tomlinson is looking at me curiously. 'Your Chief didn't say anything to you, then? And you obviously don't remember what happened at the time the shed was being built.'

'My Chief said you'd tell me.'

'He did? All right, Billy. D'you remember Jim Mallory's wife?'

'Oh, yes. I thought she was the most beautiful creature I'd ever seen. And I think even as a child I half wondered how she and Mr Mallory—'

'I suspect we all did. Although they seemed happy enough. You don't remember—'

'She went away!' Another gush of memory. 'I remember asking my grandmother why we never saw Mrs Mallory any more, and she told me she'd gone away. When I asked why, my grandmother said it was none of our business. And once I met Mr Mallory on the steps and he looked as if he'd been crying. That shocked me, I'm surprised I've only just remembered.'

'I expect there's a lot more you'll remember as the inquiry goes on. Do you remember when Jo Mallory disappeared?'

'No?'

'I do. Because I remember saying to Jim it was a pity the shed had just been finished, otherwise he could have worked some of his worry off on it.'

Fred Tomlinson and I stare at one another in silence.

The Liverpool team have found Jim Mallory. His wife never came back and he didn't marry again. He's just retired from teaching and lives in a thirties semi in the suburbs of Woolton with an Old English sheepdog. The place isn't as untidy as I was expecting, but he tells me as he lets me in that he's got a good daily whose husband looks after the garden.

He's still tall and thin with wild hair and big spectacles. All that seems to have changed is that the hair now starts a lot further back, but I wouldn't have known him, I suppose because I remember him as a type rather than an individual. He seems greatly affected by our meeting.

'Billy Jenkins! Come in, come in!' His

handclasp is painful. The dog wags its tail. 'I'm glad to see you, although I know this isn't a social call. But you'll have a coffee?'

'Thanks.' In the normal way I'd refuse, but the situation isn't normal and anyway, all we've got against him at the moment is coincidence.

'Come into the kitchen. The daily's been today so it's all right.' He looks vaguely about him, as if the kitchen belongs to someone else. The dog collapses into a corner. 'I know why you're here, of course, you don't have to tell me.'

'That makes things easier.' He puts a couple of mugs on the kitchen table, so I sit down on a kitchen chair. 'Did you ever hear from your wife, Mr Mallory?'

'Never.' His back's towards me as he takes a milk bottle out of the fridge. 'She just wasn't there when I got back from school one day, and...that was it.' He's turned to stare at me with huge shocked eyes, as if it's just happened. The Chief told me that he always used to produce the school plays, so perhaps he's an actor, too.

'No note.'

I wouldn't have thought the anguish could intensify, but it does. 'Yes. It just said...it said "Sorry, Jim. Don't look for me, I'll be all right." I know it by heart.'

'My Chief didn't show it to me.'

'I threw it away.' Helplessly he shrugs, then pours steaming water on to the instant coffee in the mugs. 'Milk?'

'Please.'

He applies it to both mugs and sits down. 'I couldn't bear to read it, and if I'd kept it I'd have been reading it all the time.'

'Yes. You didn't report her disappearance?'

'Of course not. With a note like that.'

'No, of course not.' If the note had existed. He's looking the way he looked that time I passed him on the steps and thought he'd been crying. I'm just as embarrassed as I was then, but now it's because of what I have to say. 'I believe all the men in the flats worked on the shed, Mr Mallory. Took it in turns.'

'That's right.' He stares at me defiantly, pushing his spectacles up his nose.

'At what stage was the floor laid?'

'At the end. When the roof was on. I didn't work on the floor, my last stint was the roof.'

'Who did work on the floor?'

'One of the other men, I suppose. There were three I think apart from Fred Tomlinson and me, but I can't remember.'

'Although you remember it wasn't you.

106

No professional builders among you?'

'No. But someone's brother-in-law—I think it was a brother-in-law—gave us advice.' Jim Mallory takes a gulping breath. 'Billy—Inspector—they made me look at it. They made me look at a skeleton they said was Jo!'

'But you knew it wasn't Jo. That should have made it easier.'

'Of course it wasn't Jo! Jo was alive and well when she left the Avenue. Anyway, the teeth were wrong. Oh, God,' He's staring through me in horror at his latest bad memory.

'A pity we can't trace your wife's dental records. The dentist you both went to then retired years ago, and his successors don't keep records of ex-patients as old as your wife's.'

'Oh, I know.' He slops the mug down on the table and plunges his large hands between his knees, rocking backwards and forwards. 'It's a nightmare, Billy, but it's only coincidence. What can the police do to me on the strength of coincidence?'

That's my word, but at the moment it's the only one possible. 'We can't do anything.' Unlike the Press. If—when—the Press get hold of it, Jim Mallory's life won't be worth living. All right, perhaps, if he's guilty. 'Mr Mallory, was your wife's hair naturally blonde?'

107

'It had been. She helped it along. Why do you—'

'Forgive me, but for the moment I'm asking the questions. Did her disappearance...'

'Departure.'

'Very well, departure. Did your wife's departure take you absolutely by surprise? Hadn't you any idea at all that something was wrong?'

His eyes drop to the table. 'Of course I had. I knew from the start that she didn't...love me. She was fond of me, she liked me, I was one of her lame ducks, the one that took unfair advantage of her weakness for picking them up. I hoped it would turn into something like the feeling I had for her but it didn't. She was always good and kind to me, but she must have met someone normal.'

'Not normal, perhaps. Why, if she stayed alive and well, didn't she ask you for a divorce?'

His shrug turns into a shudder. 'I don't know. I wondered. A few months after she went I wondered myself into a nervous breakdown. Oh, I've told your lot, given chapter and verse about the hospital and the convalescent home. It took me a long time to come round.'

Grief or guilt? It'll be monstrous if we never find out.

The Chief's team have traced the people still extant who were living in the flats when the shed was built—a married couple and a widow in sheltered housing and one ancient lady in a nursing-home. The ancient lady lived underneath my grandmother and was very severe, but I don't remember the other three. They remember me as the only child about the place and the man, a jolly old chap with a big red face, admits to helping lay the part of the shed floor nearest the door. But he doesn't remember who laid the back part covering the skeleton, and the ancient lady doesn't remember anything at all. When I asked the widow if she remembers anything odd about Jim Mallory's behaviour just then, she said no, because Jim Mallory was odd all the time.

None of them have sparked my memory, yet I'm feeling more and more strongly that there's something in it I'm not managing to get hold of. So the Chief has suggested it might help if I have the key to my grandmother's flat while the couple who now live there are away on their summer holidays. He's already asked them, and they've said that if it will assist the police they'll be only too pleased...

It's the longest long shot I've heard of in the whole of my career, but although we're investigating, as we must, the past of the extant husband, there doesn't seem any other place to go.

I've come straight from work, dumped my briefcase in the sitting-room, and gone out the back through the kitchen and down the stencilled iron staircase to the ground. For a moment on the staircase I thought the hollow sound my feet made was releasing more memory, but it's still out of reach.

The skeleton has held up the making of the new garden. Although all the fences have gone the site's still mostly churned soil where the police have been digging. I stumble across it to the remains of the shed: a pile of bricks and a square of broken up concrete. It's not roped off now, the police have finished with it. They didn't find anything else.

I wander about the ruin but it doesn't do anything for me. Perhaps I wasn't there when the shed was finished off.

But that figure in the dusk...

In front of the ruin I turn and look back at the flats. Three tiers of hall and dining-room windows, double oblongs of frosted glass hiding lavatories and bathrooms, small open spaces outside back doors for hanging washing... I'm learning something, I'm learning at least that I'm in the wrong place, that I should be indoors, and I go through the nearest entry to the front of the building and up the concrete steps between the three tiers of bay windows, brushing the goldenrod with my fingertips before letting myself back in through the front door.

I'm in the sitting-room now, missing my grandmother and the ticking of her clock. I've had a meat pie and a bottle of beer and faced the fact that if my instincts don't do anything for me now they never will—it's the right time of year and soon it will be the right time of day for what could be my one vital memory. If nothing happens I'll go across to Mr Tomlinson for another chat.

I'm trying to practise self-hypnosis, fill the space around me with the things that would hurt me if they were really here, recapture a child's perceptions. The dusk helps, it's darkening the furniture and the paint. I'm getting up now, letting my feet take me across the hall into the dining-room. I'm crouching down to peer out of the window from a ten-year-old height.

And the figure is there with its back to me, stumbling past my grandmother's garden with the sack in its arms. A sack of cement, they're going to mix it on the bit of hard-standing outside the door of the shed, which is finished now except for the floor...

I knock sharply on the dining-room

window, wanting the figure to turn and acknowledge me, see how grown up I am, not yet in bed. A nod of the head will do, seeing that its hands are full.

No response, so I knock again. I want the figure to turn round.

Please turn round. For God's sake turn round!

It does. And nods to me before carrying on and disappearing with the sack inside the shed.

I rang the Liverpool CS to congratulate him on his lateral thinking and ask him to give priority to a search for another dental record. I apologised for probably sending his force on a wild goose chase, but he said he would take the risk, and ordered me to go home.

I didn't hear from him for two days, then this morning he rang to tell me they'd been lucky, and I'd been right, and now I'm on my way back to the Avenue.

Mr Tomlinson comes promptly to his front door. 'Billy, how nice to see you! I saw you over the way the other night, and was disappointed you didn't call. Coffee? Are you getting anywhere?'

'No coffee, thank you, but yes, we're getting somewhere. We've arrived, in fact. We've been fortunate enough to have been able to trace your wife's dental records from the time she lived here, and they fit the teeth of the skeleton found under the floor of the shed. Sit down, Mr Tomlinson. While we're waiting for my colleagues you might like to tell me how you did it.'

I'm alarmed for a moment, he's gone so white, but the next minute he's sitting in his chair and smiling at me.

'I think I would, Billy, it's been a burden. I've had a long innings. I suppose you remembered seeing me.'

'Yes. Did you hate her that much?'

'No. But I didn't like her and I loved Jo Mallory.'

'Jo—Mallory?' The other woman with dyed blonde hair. There are a few dyed blonde hairs attached to the skull.

'She loved me, too. We worked it out together. She left the flats the day after our farewell party, the day Eunice left. Eunice and I left together, but I was only taking her to the train, I was coming back to tidy things up, honour my last stint on the shed. She never caught the train, Billy, but Jo did, and went up to Aberdeen and my new flat as Mrs Tomlinson. Just before Eunice and I left I gave Eunice some coffee that had her asleep before she had time to ask me why we were going to Formby Woods, and then it was easy.'

He smiles at me invitingly, but I decide to wait until my colleagues arrive before

113

asking him how he killed her. 'You put her in a sack...'

'Yes. A hessian one first, then one of the cement ones. I took it out to the shed that night. When I was halfway there I heard the knocking and almost had a heart attack—the landing and dining-room windows are the only ones that overlook the gardens, and it was time for curtains to be drawn. And then I saw it was just a little boy.'

'My grandmother had sent me into the dining-room to draw the curtains. I took my time because I didn't want to go to bed.'

'Even if it had been an adult I really oughtn't to have worried. Everyone knew I was going to do my last stint on the shed as well as wind things up in Liverpool before finally being on my way. It was easy, Billy, it hardly took any time to settle the sack into a shallow soil grave and cover it with the hardcore we'd got piled up inside. Then first thing the next morning I mixed enough cement to cover the back half of the shed floor. And called on Jim Mallory to say goodbye and coax out his confession that his wife had left him.

He cocks his head at me, smiling again—he smiles too much—and I say "Go on."

'It was easy all the way. Jo was a lot

slimmer than Eunice but she was roughly her height and hair colour, and she just stepped into Eunice's shoes—not literally, Billy, Scottish charities did well—learned her signature, took over her bank account, got a passport in her name—Eunice had never wanted to go abroad, but Jo and I had some good holidays. We didn't stay long in the flat I'd rented, we bought a house and didn't leave a forwarding address.'

'And didn't feel afraid?'

'Oh yes, we did, Billy. Since killing Eunice we've been afraid the whole time. Of meeting someone who knew either or both of us, of coming back to Liverpool, of being included in other people's photographs. I've even been afraid of taking my own. I wanted to photograph Jo, of course, but I never did, I turned to animals and landscapes.'

'You could put a landscape up in here.'

'I keep meaning to, and then I can't be bothered—my life ended in Scotland, Billy, when Jo died. Héloïse and Abelard. Hero and Leander. It was the love of the century.'

His eyes burn through me, I think he believes it.

'They didn't kill to be together.' But what's the use? 'Why did you come back, Fred?'

'Like I said, I'm a Liverpudlian. And part of me never left, part of me was always looking at that shed, waiting to learn that it had been demolished. When Jo died I felt I could cope with it better on the spot, as well as being in the right place, if the skeleton was discovered, to start telling the police right away about Jim Mallory's wife disappearing when she did.'

'You don't feel...badly about Jim Mallory, Fred? Or your wife?'

'Badly, Billy?' His smile mocks my repugnance. 'I just feel tired.'

'The arresting officer will be here any moment. Is there anything else you'd like to say to me before he arrives?'

'I'd like you to have a drink with me, Billy.' He struggles to his feet and goes over to a table where there's a sherry decanter and some glasses. 'Just for old time's sake.' He pours two small glasses and holds one out to me.

'Thank you, Fred, but I'd rather not.' There's something too feverishly bright and intense about his eyes. 'Please go ahead yourself, though.'

'I will, Billy.' He keeps the glass I've refused in his hand. 'I'm sorry you're not joining me, you deserve to. Cheers!' He raises the glass to me, then drinks. 'You see, Billy, I still take photographs...'

He falls against the table, and from there

to the ground, and I smell the dreaded smell. My own legs are too weak to take me along the hall to the middle bedroom to see if he's using it as a darkroom like he did thirty years ago, when he made the child promise always to wash its hands after touching anything...

I'm doing something I've never done before, I'm sitting inside one of those pubs on the long road into Liverpool from my grandmother's, giving myself a restorative scotch.

And thinking that we'll never know now how Fred Tomlinson killed his wife, seeing that her skeleton can't tell us, either.

5

The Boxer
by
MARTIN EDWARDS

'Hey man,' said Sylvester Page, 'you think I'd make a good detective?'

Harry Devlin stared at his client.

'Forget it,' he said finally. 'Mike Tyson would be more credible as a monk.'

Sylvester laughed and Harry thought he could feel the whole of the office building shake. During his time in the boxing ring, Sylvester had been two hundred and forty pounds of muscle and sinew; his manager had trumpeted him as Liverpool's Black Giant. The three years since his last bout had not been kind to him. He was running to fat and poor enough to qualify for legal aid. Yet still the sight of his huge fist smacking against his thigh made Harry wince at the imagined pain.

'Listen,' said Sylvester, 'losin' a job can turn any man to crime. I'm under Monique's feet all day at home and it's drivin' her crazy. I wouldn't want to see the inside of Walton Jail again. So why don't I do the other thing? As a kid I always dreamed of being a private eye.'

'Sam the Spade?'

Sylvester guffawed again. 'Trouble is my business, man. You've got the idea. What d'you reckon?'

'What do you know about detective work?'

'Hey, I've been a security guard for the past two years. And being a detective is mostly—what do they call it?—surveillance, ain't it?'

Harry rubbed his jaw. He could tell that, for all the banter, Sylvester was in earnest and so he wanted to keep a straight face. Yet he found it impossible to visualise his client making discreet enquiries or shadowing a suspect without bringing traffic to a standstill. Sylvester was as subtle as a Scud missile and potentially as lethal. He was by no means stupid and had the sharp sense of humour that seems to be part of every Scouser's genetic code. Yet there was an innocence about him, and an unexpected air of vulnerability, that had always appealed to Harry. It would come as no surprise to learn that Sylvester still believed in Father Christmas; disillusioning him would be as cruel as telling a child the truths of life a moment too soon.

'I'll have a word with the local enquiry agencies if you like. In the meantime, let's get on with your claim for compensation.'

'I want to sue them bastards who sacked me for every penny they've got!'

'You should get a few quid, anyway. The company says you're redundant, but it sounds like an unfair dismissal. Security's the one industry in Liverpool that is always on the up and up. Besides, they took on someone new to do your job the week after you were paid off. Let's see what the industrial tribunal makes of that, if we can't settle out of court.'

Privately, he thought a deal certain. No-one would relish confronting Sylvester in belligerent mood. His temper was awesome when roused. In the city people still remembered what he had done as a young man to the Scottish heavyweight who had incautiously larded his pre-fight press conference with a smattering of racist remarks. After three rounds, the Aberdeen Adonis looked more like a battered Bootle bag lady.

'This new director they brought in from down South kicked me out,' Sylvester complained. 'The foreman knew my story, but as soon as the other feller found out I'd done time, there was nothin' down for me.'

Harry could understand it in a way. To employ a security guard with a criminal record seemed like a contradiction in terms. Yet any villain smarter than a slab of cement would think twice about making a move on a site where Sylvester was on patrol.

A cynic might add that Sylvester had the advantage of knowing how burglars think, but the charge that he had been involved in the clumsy and abortive raid on a bank in Derby Square had been dropped through lack of evidence. If Sylvester had been able to resist the temptation to lash out at a policeman who had poured scorn on his alibi, he would never have finished up in prison.

That attack had signalled the end of his career as a bruiser, both inside and out of the ring. He'd sworn in future to go straight and so far he'd kept his word. Harry hated the thought that unemployment might provoke him to break it.

'What will you do until you get fixed up?'

'Go shootin', maybe.' Sylvester roared with merriment when he saw the alarm in his solicitor's eyes. 'Nah, don't worry. See, my cousin Earl gave me one of his guns. He spends his spare time pottin' rabbits out Halewood way.'

Harry had met Earl. He was a second hand car dealer and the obliging provider of Sylvester's alibi for the bank caper; he was said himself to have a season ticket for the Liverpool Crown Court. His excuse for owning guns was likely to be as genuine as a prostitute's smile.

'What about having another try at an ordinary job? Never mind this idea about becoming a private eye. You may well find something. People remember your name...'

'Yeah, but they want an autograph, not to give me a pay cheque. This is Liverpool, man. Jobs are as rare as Conservatives in Kirby, you know that.'

'Fair enough, but keep your ears open. Don't sit back and wait for the compensation to roll in. Roulette's a safer bet than relying on a tribunal case.'

'Okay, okay. I know what you mean. I can't spend the rest of my life watching thrillers on TV. Monique calls me the Olympic Torch, 'cause I never go out. She keeps on at me to get off my butt and find somethin'.'

His voice softened, as it always did, when he spoke about his wife. Harry had met her at their wedding eighteen months earlier. Monique was a beautiful honey-skinned girl and it was easy to understand Sylvester's devotion to her.

'Is she still working for Freddie Cork?'

'Nah. I wouldn't let any wife of mine work. That's for the man to do. The woman's job is to look after the home and him.'

Harry let that one pass by. He wasn't brave enough to argue about sexual stereotyping with a man who could reduce him to blood, skin and bone in a couple of minutes.

'She was a personal secretary, wasn't she?' he asked, choosing his words with care. 'Perhaps to tide you over she could...'

Sylvester banged his fist on the desk between them. It was a gesture of emphasis rather than of anger, yet the crack of splintering wood made Harry shudder.

'No way. When I got the elbow, she offered to go back to Freddie, but I said no fear. She even mentioned he might be willing to offer me somethin'. I told her, I wouldn't work for him again if it was the last job on earth. Not for that creep with his white suits and his Ray-Bans.'

It was an apt description of a slick businessman who had made his fortune transporting wages from banks to factories in Merseyside's bandit country in the days before cashless pay become the norm. Now Cork ran a safe deposit business in the city centre, looking after jewellery owned by plump matrons and cash that people had forgotten to record in their tax returns. Sylvester had driven security vans for him briefly; that was how the big man had first met Monique. But shortly afterwards he'd been arrested in connection with the bank robbery and Cork had seized the opportunity to sack him.

'Think about it. Good money's hard to come by.'

Sylvester grinned. 'You got it wrong. Easy to come by, hard to keep.'

True enough in his case. He'd never made it to the top in boxing, no doubt due in part to the failings of his manager, who was the sort who would have told John Lennon to go back to Art School and recommended his clients to put their shirts on a 100-1 shot in the Grand National. But there was something missing in Sylvester's own make-up as well. He had the power and the skill, but what he lacked, Harry thought, was the killer instinct. There was a warmth about him which the best boxers did without. His naïveté was as endearing as his willingness to use humour against himself. Those were not qualities Freddie Cork shared—but Cork was a rich man, a winner, and Sylvester no more than a fallen idol, overweight and out of work.

Rising to his feet, Harry said, 'I'll send the papers in to the tribunal. Good luck down the mean streets.'

Sylvester offered a huge paw, but Harry evaded it. After the last time they'd shaken hands, he had not been able to grip a ballpoint pen for a week.

When the boxer had gone, Harry ambled into Jim Crusoe's office. His partner was a fight fan and the two of them had once watched Sylvester do battle at the Silk House Sporting Club. The sight of two men trying to knock hell out of each other for money had left Harry cold.

'Sylvester Page has been sacked. I've been advising on a tribunal claim. He sent you his regards.'

'How is he?'

Harry shrugged. 'Down but not out, same as in that scrap we saw at the Silk House. He's even talking of becoming a private detective.'

Jim gazed at the heavens. 'Lacking a bit in the little grey cells, isn't he?'

'I didn't want to discourage him,' said Harry. A nostalgic smile spread across his face as he added, 'Asking only workman's wages, he's gone looking for a job, but he's got no offers.'

In response to his partner's puzzled stare, he explained sheepishly, 'I was thinking of an old Simon and Garfunkel song about a boxer.'

Jim shook his head in a parody of despair.

'Never mind *The Guinness Book of Hit Singles*. Get back to *Atkin's Court Forms* and make us a few quid.'

One rainy day the following week, Harry

125

met Sylvester coming out of a doorway in Brunswick Street. He glanced up at the sign above the front window of the building. It bore the legend WILLING HANDS.

'So you're still looking, then? Sorry I couldn't come up with anything for you in the gumshoe line.'

Sylvester made as if to slap him playfully on the back, but Harry skipped out of range like a neurotic Gene Kelly.

'You told me to get off my ass. Well, that's what I done. Monique spotted this ad in the paper, she said it was worth givin' a go.'

'Any joy?'

'Man, they tell me this job has my name on it. Great hours, even better money. And no sweat.'

'Where can I apply?'

'Somehow I don't think you qualify, Harry.'

'So what exactly are you going in for?'

A coy look flitted across Sylvester's face. 'That'd be tellin'.'

Harry's suspicions were aroused. Whilst he found it hard to imagine Willing Hands advertising anything illegal in the Press, little would surprise him about the branch boss, Edie Brailsford. He had once acted for her, in the days when she was manageress of an escort agency which had fallen foul of the police because of the eagerness of its young ladies to keep their customers satisfied. To everyone's amazement, when her case came to court, she was found not guilty. Harry still wondered if she might have enjoyed a previous business acquaintance with one of the magistrates.

'Suit yourself,' he said reluctantly. 'I'll be in touch when I have news about your claim.'

Sylvester turned up the collar of his raincoat in the manner of an outsize Columbo and headed into Drury Lane, leaving Harry to scan the recruitment agency's window. It was impossible not to admire the skill with which a handful of vacancy cards were arranged so as to give the impression that Liverpool was a hotbed of opportunity for the vocationally challenged.

'Harry, sweetheart! Looking for a Willing Girl?'

A middle-aged woman wearing a tight sweater and too much make-up had put her head round the door of the agency. The arching of her pencilled eyebrows gave her an expression of permanent innuendo.

'Hello, Edie. Matter of fact, I've just been talking to a client of yours. Sylvester Page.'

'Isn't he a hunk?'

127

'He seems happy enough with the job you've found him. What is it, exactly?'

Edie Brailsford gave a mischievous smile. 'Now that would be telling. You'll understand, sweetheart, as a fellow professional, that we have to observe strict client confidentiality. My good name depends upon it.'

So far as Harry was concerned, Edie's good name was Loretta Labelle, the alias by which the escort agency's clients had known her, but he didn't press his questions. A vague idea was forming in his mind that he might not appreciate the answers.

Yet over the next few days, he often found himself wondering what Sylvester was up to, and his curiosity was given a further tweak the following Monday.

He had been over in Birkenhead interviewing a client and he'd taken the underground train rather than bothering to drive. When he arrived back at James Street station, he ignored the lift and chose to climb the long sloping ramp which led to the Water Street exit. It was a nod to keep-fit which would make him feel less guilty about having a couple of Mars bars instead of lunch.

He emerged panting into the open air and, hurrying across the road with his head down, he cannoned into a human Himalaya standing on the edge of the pavement opposite the station entrance.

'Hey, are you okay?' asked Sylvester Page.

What little breath Harry had left had been knocked out of him and a few seconds passed before he was able to reply.

'I'll live, probably. God knows what it feels like to be hit by you when you really mean to hurt. Anyway, I thought you would have started work by now.'

Sylvester beamed. 'Started already, haven't I?'

He was wearing a baseball cap of the type once sported by the late Robert Maxwell and a lime-green shell suit too small for his enormous frame. It was the kind of outfit that caused Harry to suspect that Sylvester had learned to box in order to teach a lesson to all the other kids who mocked his taste in clothes.

'Don't tell me that is your working uniform.'

'Nice, innit? Got style. Anyway, they let me choose my own gear. Perk of the job.'

'Oh yes, the mysterious job. Are you going to tell me what it is?'

A broad grin spread across Sylvester's face. He raised a finger to his lips.

'Got to keep mum, haven't I? Can't talk about it at all, it's more than my job's worth. Know what I mean, Harry?'

Harry gave up and said goodbye. But as he walked up Water Street, a thought occurred to him. He glanced over his shoulder and saw that Sylvester had scarcely moved. The big man was peering into the window of a building society. It was difficult to believe that he had a genuine interest in premium share accounts and offshore tax investments. If the idea was not absurd, Harry would have said Sylvester was trying to fade into the scenery.

Harry crossed the road again. Buses tailing back from the traffic lights opposite the Liver Building blocked him from his client's view. He stopped outside the building which occupied the corner of Water Street and Drury Lane, opposite the accountants' office which Harry had once visited in search of the explanation of his wife's murder.

A short flight of stone steps led up to a huge metal door. Beside the door a discreet brass plate bore the legend *Liverpool Safe Deposit Company*.

For all the brightness of the sunshine, Harry felt a sudden chill. Might Sylvester be carrying out—to use his own word—surveillance on the premises of his former employer? And if so—what could be the reason for it?

When Harry reached his office a minute later, he found waiting for him a new client, a man in his mid-forties so squat and ugly he might have been designed by the architect of a sixties' housing estate. Whilst he advised on how to sue the dating agency which had failed to find his client a woman desperate enough for marriage, Harry puzzled over the mystery of Sylvester's new job. As soon as he had dispatched the disappointed suitor, he dialled Sylvester's home number and drummed his fingers impatiently on the desk until at last a woman's voice answered.

'Monique, it's Harry Devlin here. Sorry to disturb you. I bumped into Sylvester half an hour ago, but I forgot to ask him for information about his new job. It may affect his unfair dismissal claim, and his likely compensation.'

'I don't know much about it,' said Monique. She seemed to be choosing her words with care. 'Shall I ask him to ring you?'

He wondered about the reason for her guarded tone. In the past he had always found her open and chatty. As a guest at their wedding, he remembered envying Sylvester his good fortune. But Monique was shrewd too, and she knew he shared her husband's fondness for playing the detective. Instinctively he sensed she was anxious to keep something from him.

'Any idea when he's due in?'

'Let's see. It's two fifteen now. Maybe around quarter to six.'

'I'm glad he's fixed up,' said Harry quickly. He could tell she was about to hang up. 'But do you think he's happy in this new job?'

'Of course! It suits him perfectly.'

Harry thought she was protesting too much. He determined to press further.

'Do you know who he's working for?'

'It's...it's all supposed to be hush-hush.'

'Look, I'm on Sylvester's side, remember.'

'Well...he's been hired to do some detective work.'

'Sylvester?'

Harry didn't pretend to hide his amazement.

'Yes—and why not?'

'Come on, I love him dearly, you're well aware of that. But we can be frank with each other.' He swallowed. Never mind frankness, it was time to be bloody rude. 'And the truth is, I wouldn't back him to find a needle in a sewing shop.'

'You underestimate him,' she said angrily. 'I thought you were his friend.'

He was in too deep now to draw back.

'Monique, has he got mixed up with something shady?'

'I told you! He's taken a job as a private investigator. Now, I'm really busy and I'm surprised you seem to have time to waste instead of pushing on with Sylvester's case.'

She slammed the phone down, leaving Harry alone with his speculations.

No-one in their right mind, surely, would pay Sylvester to act the sleuth. All the local firms Harry had spoken to had dismissed out of hand the idea of offering the man a job. If they were looking for new recruits at all, they would find them in the ranks of ex-policemen, not former boxers with a criminal past.

Since the encounter in Water Street, an unwelcome suspicion had been loitering in Harry's mind like a grubby squatter to whom he could no longer deny house room. He groaned, and the noise attracted the attention of Jim Crusoe, who had been passing the door.

Looking in, Jim said, 'What's eating you? Anyone would think you'd just been asked to serve a writ on a rottweiler.'

'I'm bothered about Sylvester. I'm inclined to think old habits are dying hard.'

He gave an account of his conversations with Sylvester and Monique. His partner listened intently.

'So what do you make of it?'

'One thing's for sure, Sylvester is no more a Poirot than Bertie Wooster was a Hell's Angel.'

'What, then?'

'Twice now I've seen him in the vicinity of the place where he used to work, the Liverpool Safe Deposit Company. There's no love lost between him and Freddie Cork. He's been on the fringe of an armed robbery in the past. His cousin Earl must merit his own special floppy disc in the Police National Computer. He's in possession of a gun. And Monique appears to be covering for him.'

'You don't suppose he's planning some sort of raid on the safe deposits?'

'You're more of a shamus than Sylvester will ever be. You got it in one.'

'So what can you do? Tip off the police?'

'What kind of solicitor grasses on his own client? Especially a client who's an old pal and hasn't committed a crime?'

'Will you have a word with him, then?'

'No alternative, is there? I wonder if he's still hopping round outside that building society. It must dawn soon even on him that he sticks out there like snow in the Sahara.'

He walked round to the place where he had last spoken to Sylvester. This time there was no sign of the big man on

134

either side of the road. The way in to James Street railway station, he observed, was barred by a grille. Curious, he thought. At this time of day there was usually open access to the ramp.

He walked up to the grille and read the notice attached to it.

Station closed this afternoon due to industrial action. Merseyrail apologises for any inconvenience caused.

He turned into Drury Lane and bought an early edition of the local paper.

'What's happened at the station?' he asked the news vendor.

'Another of these lightning strikes,' he was told. 'No warning at all. One minute the trains were coming through. Next minute they stopped.'

His next port of call was the Willing Hands agency. There he found Edie flirting with a job seeker young enough to be her son. Perhaps even, he thought ungallantly, her grandson.

'Sorry to interrupt, but I need to contact Sylvester Page. Sooner rather than later.'

Edie frowned. The job seeker took the hint and sloped off.

'I told you, sweetheart, it's confidential. Professional ethics, you know.'

'Look, I wouldn't persist if it wasn't important. Besides, you still owe me a favour after the Pretty Partners case. I've

135

already worked out this job of Sylvester's is a charade, but I'm hoping you'll be able to give me a clue to what is really going on.'

Edie pursed her lips, but nonetheless she waved him into her private cubicle at the back of the open plan office. Once inside she reached for a card index box from which she drew a paper oblong.

'Here.'

Harry read the closely printed card with astonishment. A client had asked Willing Hands to find him a private detective. The candidate had to meet certain requirements. He or she must be free to take up the post at once, without having to give notice to a current employer. He or she must have experience of the security industry, be physically fit and have proven skill in the art of self-defence. And he or she must have been born and bred within one mile of the Liver Building.

'My client doesn't want much, does he?' asked Edie. 'I never knew anyone so pernickety. Told me which local paper to advertise in and then insisted I interview the candidates myself. I had a set of sealed orders I was supposed to give to the right person. I said to my client, you'll be lucky, you'll never find anyone to fit this bill.'

Harry gnawed at his fingernails. He was thinking furiously.

'Oh yes, very confident he was,' continued Edie. 'A fool and his money are soon parted, I thought. Yet lo and behold, who should turn up straight away but your mate Sylvester. Miracles do happen after all, I said to myself.'

'I don't think there was anything miraculous about it,' said Harry slowly.

'What are you getting at?'

'Who was your client?'

Edie drew herself up. 'Sorry, but I reckon I've repaid that favour. My integrity...'

Harry scribbled a name on the card and tossed it back to her.

'Am I right?'

She gaped at him. 'Well, as a matter of fact...'

'Did you happen to see what was in the sealed orders?'

Edie twittered something about the glue on the envelope coming unstuck and the papers falling out. Harry interrupted in the middle of her self-justification.

'Did they say anything about keeping an eye on the Water Street entrance to Merseyrail between, say, specified hours of the afternoon?'

She shook her head in bafflement. 'How do you know all this?'

'I read minds, Edie. Trouble is, I was dyslexic to begin with. Thanks for your help. Mind if I use your phone?'

He dialled a number but couldn't get through. The receiver had been taken off the hook.

Without another word, he left. Time was short, that he knew. Sylvester lived in the inner city; the best hope was that he had not gone straight home when the railways had closed down unexpectedly.

He hurried round the corner to where he parked his MG convertible and within a minute was heading down the Strand towards the block of flats where the Pages had their home. As he drove, he cursed himself for being no less naïve than his client.

He pressed the accelerator, praying he would not be too late.

As he swung into a side road, a ten storey tower loomed above him. He was still praying he would not be too late when he caught sight of something flying from a top floor window. All he could see was a white blur in the air for a split second before it hit the ground.

He stamped on the brakes and pulled up thirty yards from the block. By the time he got there, people who had come running from the street were gathering around the broken body on the tarmac. Craning his neck to see beyond them, he caught a glimpse of naked flesh, tightly permed hair and a pool of blood.

At first he thought his legs would give way beneath him. On the way here, he had clung to the hope that his guesswork might be wildly wrong, but the evidence that his worst fears had been well-founded lay on the ground in front of him.

'Not a stitch on him,' said a woman in curlers. Her voice was dazed, but fascinated.

'Call an ambulance,' wheezed an asthmatic old man with a *Daily Mirror* tucked under his arm.

'Don't you mean the road sweeper?' asked a leather-jacketed youth with a sickly smile.

His heart pounding, Harry forced himself to stumble towards the tall building. Whether he could salvage anything from the disaster now he doubted, but he knew he must try.

To his amazement, the lift was working and the car was at the ground floor, ready and waiting for him. It's a sign, he thought, there is still a chance.

As he pressed the button marked 10, he asked himself how long the affair had been going on. Anything to take his mind off that mess of death on the road outside.

For all he knew, the relationship between Monique Page and Freddie Cork was a recent thing. But even if it dated back to the time when she had worked for him, Sylvester's redundancy must have been unwelcome. With her man hanging around home all day, every day, Monique had little opportunity to misbehave.

The lovers needed Sylvester to get out of the house and they had to know how much time they could spend together, secure in the knowledge that they would not be disturbed. Concocting the job of Sylvester's dreams must have seemed like a perfect solution: it made everyone happy. The job description had been devised with Sylvester's personal curriculum vitae in mind. The details of the sealed cock-and-bull story instructing him to watch for a mythical quarry didn't matter. The key point was that, from his office window, Cork could see that the cuckold had taken up the appointed position and would know that he was safe to slip out by a side door and speed over here to his lover's open arms.

But he had not counted on a snap rail strike and on Sylvester deciding that as there was no point in staying on duty, he might as well go home.

To be interrupted in a passionate embrace by a call from a nosey solicitor was bad luck; no wonder they had taken the phone off the hook. To be caught *in flagrante* by a hot-tempered husband with sledgehammer fists had, for Freddie Cork, been a fatal misfortune.

The lift reached its destination and he raced down the corridor. The Pages, he remembered, lived at the far end. But he was half a dozen strides from their front door when a single gunshot rang out. It was followed by a scream that Harry thought would never end.

For perhaps one whole minute he stood transfixed. Not for the first time in his life he was swamped by a sense of loss. The pain, he knew from past experience, would come later. For now there was nothing but a feeling of utter helplessness.

He trudged to the door of the Pages' flat. It was open and from the passageway he could see through into the living room.

Sylvester's corpse lay on the floor, directly below a cluster of photographs on the wall which showed him winning fights and having his arm raised aloft in triumph by midget referees. Harry gagged at the sight of the bloody remains of what had once been his client's head. Earl's gun lay where it had fallen on the carpet.

A couple of feet away, Monique crouched in a foetal ball, rocking backwards and forwards with her head in her hands. She had stopped screaming and was now making a keening sound. She was naked, as she must have been when her husband arrived home before he was due.

Sylvester had got it wrong, thought Harry. He'd wanted to be a Merseyside Marlowe and had finished up more like Moose Malloy.

He closed his eyes in a vain attempt to shut out the horror, but the ghastly sound of the wailing widow went on and on. In his misery he realised that he too had been mistaken. His client had not, after all, lacked the killer instinct.

6

Home Ground
by
ANDREW GARDNER

Most of us are sitting on a fortune of information and experience perfect for any novel. It may be a case of failing to see the woods because the trees get in the way. Possibly we feel we lead less glamorous lives and do not have such heady occupations as others.

In my own particular case, I 'discovered', rather than being told directly that I was surrounded, not always by plots, but by settings and situations ideal for any writer.

This I owe to author Bruce Crowther, who has also written under the name of James Grant. In conversation I was told a publisher was not looking for a book. It was more complicated than that. A publisher wants books. A publisher wants a novel that can be filmed, televised, serialised, even so far as the location and main characters being used in a series written by others. And the cost, for an

143

unknown writer, is a weighty matter.

An industrial estate, a British town, a British port and the like are not especially exotic but they are there and easy to get to—and therefore cheap.

I've never worked as a lumberjack, I've never set foot on an offshore drilling platform and I've never flown a supersonic aircraft. What I have done is worked in the shipping and transport business for twenty years in the North of England and, even though the plots aren't there, the settings and a richness of background information are—when I look for them.

My home town is Goole, which has appeared one way or another in more books than you would think. However, towns change, main streets are pedestrianised, businesses move in and out, so I created an imaginary North of England port and town some fifty miles upriver from the North Sea—as is Goole.

My hero, private detective Sam Shank, is a cliché. The plot for his first appearance in print—*The Twin Bridges Murder*—was inspired by a geographical and historical peculiarity in Worksop. The creation of Sam Shank's character was slapdash. I thought the ex-copper was overdone, and I knew nothing of police procedure. But the hero needed a convincing link with the local law, so Shank's ex-wife has married a detective sergeant.

A totally lucky ploy, I discovered subsequently, was to give Shank a local background. He was a truck driver once upon a time. His widowed girl friend is a partner in a road haulage business, giving Shank access to what's going on in the town and port.

Shank's second appearance in print —*Trailersnatch!*—is only significant because great chunks of that novel were salvaged from a police story which proved to be a non-starter.

More important, to me at least, was Shank's unwilling appearance in *Rivermist*. At the time I was tired of my creation. I had seen a televised dramatisation of P.M Hubbard's *The Causeway,* and read a number of his novels. As always in his work, the landscape, beautifully described, dominates.

I wanted a situation where a quiet backwater is threatened by approaching industry. The problem was that I could not find a hero who could describe both 'sides' and remain neutral in the conflict. Although prodded by the obvious commercial reasons, it dawned on me that Sam Shank was again the right man; taken from his usual habitat with no real allegiance to either side, he made the perfect hero/narrator.

145

Rivermist, I must report, rather than boast or wonder, raised a few eyebrows amongst relatives and friends. I was not surprised at claims that the plot had been inspired by a local landmark and my own involvement with quiet river wharves.

But I was surprised by at least one claim that the plot was based on a river miles away, although in the same county. On reflection I wonder if subconscious inspiration had originated in an old painting of a tranquil river, that has been in my family for generations.

The most surprising and certainly the most indisputable claim came from my parents who, independently, reminded me of a holiday many years back when, as a child, I had stayed in an isolated area of the West Country at a farm with a river meandering by.

If any lesson is to be learnt, we all have half-forgotten memories tucked away in our minds that almost literally spring to life when needed. Thank goodness...

Although not so much cruising as on automatic pilot, I gave Sam Shank a fourth outing in a book called *Kickback.* This was a collection of gathered experience, do's and don'ts and also an interesting example of my getting a book under way despite toying mentally with a plot and being unable to find that vital opening scene.

Inspiration and salvation arrived in a most unlikely and slightly insignificant manner. A small freighter in Goole had a mechanical breakdown. Small but essential spares were urgently needed. However, this happened at a Bank Holiday, resulting in all our 'phone calls to the necessary suppliers being unanswered or, worse, being greeted with unhelpful recorded messages promising immediate attention.

Frustrating as this experience was at the time, it was the opener I needed; substituting Sam Shank into my real life shoes and having him drive over the Pennines for the necessary spares and pick up a hitch-hiker on the way back who subsequently vanished and was then found murdered. Not only was the plot, thankfully, under way but Shank was involved from the start.

Another lesson learnt, or re-learnt during the writing of *Kickback* was: if a good idea develops, use it immediately, don't save it to the last chapter.

A third of the way through *Kickback*, I made a voyage across the North Sea from Hull. The thrill of a big ship ploughing through the darkness had to be used, but sparingly. What was a new or newish experience to me was commonplace to those who made a living from the sea.

On paper, Sam Shank made two North

Sea voyages; the first authenticated Shank's abilities and the exploits on the second trip, hopefully, did not appear contrived. The reader had been there before; a situation was made to be part of the plot's development, not something seemingly snatched at.

On reflection, I realised this was a device I had used before in my first book where the final location and situation for the climax, although not visited by the hero until well on into the plot, had been mentioned previously.

By now, I was tiring slightly of Sam Shank and had realised the pitfalls and potential repetitiveness of constantly using the same main character and location. I had another hero in print by the time Shank strode out in a fifth adventure—*A Touch of Jade.*

Once again, when I was scratching around for ideas, inspiration returned in maritime form. I had been involved with a West German tug that had arrived in Goole to deal with a long-haul tow. This tug had operated in the South Atlantic and seethed power, energy and just a hint of menace. What better vehicle, or vessel, to have bringing back into Sam Shank's world someone from his past?

For me, though, Shank had been slightly eclipsed by Jack Culver, a cynical secret agent who owed not a little to Len Deighton's nameless character who became known on screen as Harry Palmer. There was also a nod, I hope respectful, in the direction of Gavin Lyall's heroes and later I discovered that I had also been unconsciously influenced by the hero of Angus Ross's many novels.

Jack Culver, unlike Shank, lived in a world where places had names. *Duckett's Condor* was set in Hull and North Humberside. A lengthy and somewhat surreal chapter where Culver, driving through the countryside at Harvest time with stubble fire smoke drifting upwards, had been contemplating D-Day with its rising smoke from knocked-out tanks and armour, was dropped.

Culver's second appearance—*Slate Secret* —was the result of a holiday in North Wales. He is a logical extension of Sam Shank, although differences appeared when Culver was afforded a walk-on part to deal with a situation in a Shank novel that Shank would not, convincingly, have undertaken.

Since most of those seven books were written, I have undertaken a job not involved in the shipping industry—at least not directly. I have become a journalist. But often the tables are turned and people ask me the question I am most often asked:

how do you become a novelist? Replies such as hard work, determination, rejection slips, disappointments and a dozen or more pitfalls are usually greeted with cynical disbelief, followed by hints that the writer is dodging the issue; there is a big secret to it all...

Well, there is a secret. Anyone can write a novel. Getting it published is another matter. But everyone has a past, experience, wishes and dreams. If mankind can land men on the moon, driving a typewriter is not too hard by comparison.

Many years ago, I studied art; not particularly successfully, but I learned how to transform a blank sheet of paper into a picture. I worked in layers, adding here, leaving out there.

I know that thrill of a ship about to sail. I know what it is like waiting for a ship to arrive in port at three o'clock on a November morning.

I don't actually know what makes a ship work, nor an aircraft, a lorry, or a train, because that was never my job. I was concerned with moving stuff from A to B by the most suitable, quickest and convenient methods available.

So are many other people. And in my neck of the woods where salt, real or imagined, flows in everyone's veins, I have to get the technical bits more or less right. And it is a simplification, but perhaps fair, to say that a writer, especially a crime writer, must be a master of understatement, capable of careful suggestion and implication.

Inspiration from other sources is rarely debated. Actual inspiration for a character hit me once when I was taking a breather from my typewriter and walking my dog.

One's home ground is important, too. I live in a busy North of England port—an ideal background for a crime writer. Having said that, it's rather strange to admit that very recently I was visiting a nearby city and in the middle of a busy street, for no obvious reason, I had an idea for a plot. Twenty-four hours later, I was in a one-time stately home—the perfect setting.

Imagination, inspiration or simple logic? The answer is probably the latter because, like everyone else, I have not only read crime novels but also read books on how to write and books on crime fiction history. Books on a variety and bewildering number of subjects, from Second World War aircraft to defunct railways, crowd my bookcase.

I drag my eyes and ears open and my mouth shut. I was once wracking my brains for a support character for one novel and found him standing in the queue at the bank within days.

I have been asked if journalism is a good fishing ground for a writer. Unless one is a foreign correspondent with ready access to faraway places, I would be wary about saying that it is.

I am now familiar with police, court and local authority procedures, but more to my immediate advantage is that I am meeting people in places and situations I never had the opportunity to encounter before.

A chance remark in a pub—where else?—has given me the idea for a plot. I would guess that anyone who writes is a person who never switches off. When writers are gathered together their senses quiver, twist and turn with that gentle grace of Tigers in the Ardennes. Unwitting and totally innocent passers-by are mentally singled out to become heroes, villains, mass murderers or chapter-one corpses.

A pleasing dawn or sunset can become the backdrop for brutal murder or swift and telling retribution. Places we pass by daily without a second glance become scenes of violence, robbery and intrigue. I once thought an out-of-season seaside resort would make a good setting for a thriller. The notion was still flowering in my brain when I discovered two novels in rapid succession where that device was employed.

But in the end it is back to home

ground. True, there are writers whose research involves many months of travel, and their diligence must not go unrewarded or unacknowledged, although I suspect these fortunate people are in a minority.

Much more numerous are those who write about places they know well, usually the towns where they live or come from. We all know that it is possible to do a thoroughly convincing job and write about a place we have never visited, although I am sure a writer sooner rather than later would feel obliged to visit the country or city in his book or books, to settle his own desire for authenticity, accuracy and—most important—atmosphere.

If there exists an unwritten golden rule to write about what you know about, I'm sure we all do well to stick to it. And that brings us back again to home ground. There is no better place.

7

Market Forces
by
REGINALD HILL

It is one thing to utter pearls of wisdom. Quite another to swallow them yourself. They tend to stick in the throat.

The pearl George Faber found himself choking on was one he had often cast before would-be entrepreneurs in his capacity as Small Business Advisor at the Cumbrian Investment Bank.

Cornering a market is pointless unless you've cracked the distribution problem.

He had been wiser than he knew, and the getting of wisdom is a great sorrow.

For he had cornered the market in dead Mrs Fabers without giving any thought at all to the problem of distributing the remains.

Of course it wouldn't have been a normal suburban marriage if during its twenty-five-year duration he hadn't occasionally fantasized about being a vigorous widower with insurance money to burn; but his earthbound imagination had never envisaged attaining that blessed state by means other than illness or accident.

In the present circumstances, *illness* was definitely out. He looked down at the body and tried *accident* for size.

'I'd been out in the garden chopping firewood, and I got rather hot so I came into the kitchen to get a beer, and Phyllis started screaming at me not to track dirt across her nice clean tiles, and then this dreadful accident happened...'

He paused hoping for inspiration but none came. Even a more creative thinker than dull old George Faber might have been hard put to it to explain how his hatchet came to be buried *accidentally* in his wife's head.

He went to the fridge, got a can of beer and drank it while he debated what to do.

Three cans later, he opted for what dull bank executives usually opt for, which is the obvious, and decided to bury her in the cellar.

It was a Cumbrian farm-house, tastefully modified by the addition of central heating, air conditioning, double glazing, sprung flooring, spot-lighting, wall-to-wall carpeting, and vibrant Provençal colouring, all without compromising its quintessential *oldness*.

Only the cellar remained untouched.

155

There had been talk of pine panels and strip lights, of flood-lit pool tables and racks of fine wine, but even Phyllis Faber's springs of inspiration dried whenever she looked into those dark, mice-infested depths. In the end it came to be used as a dumping ground for items too old for use, too familiar to throw away.

A more cynical or a more fanciful man might have been amused to place his wife's corpse in this category, but it never occurred to George.

He simply covered the body with a heavy Liberty tablecloth, wishing he'd had the foresight to lay it on the floor before he axed her, thus making it easier to wrap her up and also pre-empting the gruesome task still to come of mopping up the blood from the Tuscan tiles.

On the other hand Phyllis had been the kind of woman who noticed things like tablecloths spread across the kitchen floor. He'd wanted a carpet. He hated these cold slippery tiles. But she'd laughed him to scorn, and later tongue lashed him to tears when he'd had the effrontery to introduce a small rug as a stepping stone from the outside door to the dining room.

No more of that! He went out to his shed for a pick and shovel and did a little dusty dance across the tiles as he made for the cellar steps. The age of stockinged feet was past. From now on it was wellies, wellies, all the way!

Down in the cellar, lit by a single unshaded light bulb, he set to work.

It wasn't easy. First he had to shift the household rubbish to reveal that the floor was paved with rough hewn granite slabs. At least four of these had to be levered aside to create enough space to dig a grave. This done, he wiped the sweat from his brow and went up into the kitchen to get another beer. He drank it slowly, finding himself strangely reluctant to descend the steps again. Phyllis dead and draped with a tablecloth was only a mildly discomforting presence, but down there, out of the daylight...

He shook his head irritably. *A man in a hurry has no time to worry.* Another pearl he produced at Small Business Seminars. He crumpled his can in his hand, tossed it into the sink with the others, smiled at this sacrilege, and headed back down.

Now the real labour began. Fortunately George had kept in pretty good condition, refusing to let even an arthritic knee keep him from squash in the winter and at least a dozen sets of tennis a week throughout the summer. But he quickly realised that his sporting life had developed muscles more suited to the killing smash with a hatchet than a double handed overhead with a pick.

It occurred to him after a while (this lack of forward planning again!) that the Archimedean theory of displacement applied as much to earth as to water, and he went back upstairs to collect another couple of tablecloths to shovel soil onto.

Fortunately Phyllis had been a compulsive snapper-up of sales bargains on her trips south and the absence of a few tablecloths was unlikely to be noticed even by the most perceptive of detectives.

The thought of detectives depressed him, however, and he unzipped another can of beer. In all his fantasies, the prospect of a wifeless life had opened up before him like a sunlit landscape seen from a high terrace where he took his ease with a champagne cocktail in his hand. It had never occurred to him that beneath that terrace, dividing him from that landscape, there might be a rocky ravine of interrogation and suspicion, not to mention depression and guilt.

He shook these dark thoughts from his mind, tossed the empty can into the sink, and went back to work.

Twenty minutes later his pick drove through the packed earth and bounced back with a resounding clang. He tested to left and right with the same result. He had reached solid rock.

The hole he had so far excavated was less than three feet deep. Conventional even in these unconventional circumstances, he had been aiming at six. But now he came to think of it, the cellar steps had already taken him ten feet beneath the earth's surface, so he was way ahead of schedule.

Happy to think the worst was over, he set about shovelling the remaining loose earth onto the cloth. The bedrock thus revealed took him by surprise. It certainly wasn't granite, but more like some form of chrysoprase, highly polished so that it glowed apple green beneath the single light bulb, and smooth and as level as a ballroom floor. He could see no pock mark where his pick had impacted, and the sharp edge of his spade skidded off this surface with no hint of a scratch.

Puzzled, he touched it with his hand and drew back with an exclamation of surprise. It had that degree of coldness which almost burns like fire.

He was not by nature an inquisitive man. Professionally his strength had always been his ability to concentrate on the job in hand to the exclusion of all else. So, odd though this layer of bedrock was, his natural inclination was to collect Phyllis and get on with the task of burying her.

Instead, he found himself unwilling,

indeed perhaps unable to move. He stood there quite still, his gaze riveted on that glowing green slab.

For it was a slab, he now realised. No bedrock this, but another floor level, laid God knows how long ago and covered with the earth on which eventually his own cellar floor had been set.

'Come on, Faber!' he urged himself as though he were at a conference. 'Eye on the target. Mind on the job. You've killed your wife, you're burying her body, this is no time for archaeology.'

But still he could not move away. Instead he knelt on the slab and explored it with his fingers till he found an edge. Now working with a feverish energy which made his previous efforts seem lethargic, he began to scrape away the soil along that edge, following it round till at last he had the whole slab in outline.

It was about six feet long, three feet wide. Grave size. Had someone been here before him?

He resumed his explorations into the soil beneath the edge and quickly established that the slab was no more than two inches deep. He was able to wriggle the toe of his pick beneath it, and now he threw himself against the pick handle in an attempt to lever the slab upward.

At first it resisted his efforts with a

pressure that seemed disproportionate to its likely weight, but he soon found that he was exerting a leverage far beyond his normal strength.

For a period which seemed timeless, lever and weight seemed locked in perfect balance. Then the slab moved. Just a fraction. Just enough to open a crack between the edge and what lay beneath. But it was as if this tiny aperture acted as a vacuum release. There was a noise of inrushing air as though something down there, long deprived of oxygen, was gulping in huge breathfuls. And as the air rushed in, the slab twitched and creaked and groaned and finally flew open like the cover of a book in an explosion of earth, stone, and evil smelling dust.

George shot upright. The tip of his pick shattered the light bulb. Coughing and spluttering, he staggered to the steps and crawled up into the kitchen. Even when he felt the cool tiles under his hands, he could see very little, as the dust seemed to have come up with him. Now he got the impression that its swirlings were becoming more uniform. It was twisting in an anti-clockwise direction, like a mini-cyclone, as though driven by some centrifugal force. Not just the dust but the very air seemed to be moving and there was a noise like iron-rimmed wheels sparking across a paved courtyard.

He closed his eyes and cried aloud with fear.

When he opened them again, he found he was looking at a pair of shoes.

They were slightly pointed, highly polished and ornately knotted.

He raised his head. His gaze travelled up the knife-edge crease of a pair of elegant green trousers, traversed a saffron coloured shirt beneath a casual jacket in pale blue silk, and finally reached a face.

For a second the angle made it look like an animal's face, foxy, fanged, ferocious. He blinked, pushed himself to his knees, and saw in fact it was the face of a young man, rather narrow and a touch swarthy, but not at all frightening. In fact his features were full of concern.

'I say, are you all right?' he said anxiously.

His voice was light, lilting, with just a trace of a foreign accent.

George said, 'Yes, thanks, fine.'

He stood upright and began dusting himself down. Only there was no dust. It all seemed to have vanished.

'Who the hell are you?' George demanded with a sudden aggression provoked by the realisation that if the stranger took a couple of steps backward he would be treading on Phyllis's body.

162

'I was just passing and I heard a noise, and I wanted to be sure everything was all right. Why don't we step outside for a moment and get a breath of air? It's a bit close in here.'

George had no objection to getting out of the kitchen. Unfortunately Phyllis lay between the stranger and the door. Which meant he must have stepped over her when he came in. It didn't seem to have bothered him. He stepped over her again without even looking down and went out onto the patio. Perhaps the tented effect produced by the hatchet had misled him into thinking it covered something else, but the outline of the legs and feet was unmistakable.

Skirting the tablecloth carefully, George followed the stranger. He found him standing with his head thrown back, drawing in deep breaths, his eyes fixed on the turbulent sky. As George joined him, he made a gesture with his left hand and forearm which brought to mind a holiday in Greece when a passing truck driver had taken exception to George's driving. But this young man's attention seemed to be focused firmly on the lurid clouds bubbling over the Lakeland fells.

Suddenly he looked round, smiled in slight embarrassment and said, 'Lovely day, isn't it?'

'If that's what you like,' said George.

'Indeed. Well, if you're sure you're OK, I ought to be pushing on. Things to do.'

'I'm fine,' said George.

'Good.'

The younger man began to move away, but at the edge of the patio he hesitated and looked back.

'Is there anything I can do for you before I go?' he asked.

'I don't think so,' said George.

'Any little service. Doesn't matter what. Just name it,' insisted the young man.

'No, really,' said George. He didn't know what the fellow's game was, he just wanted rid of him.

'There has to be something,' persisted the stranger. 'I'd really like to help. Please.'

'There's absolutely nothing,' said George with some irritation. He turned away, meaning to go back into the kitchen and lock the door, but somehow his feet wouldn't work.

The stranger came and stood in front of him, very close. His breath smelt like the warm gust from the ventilator of a Thai restaurant. 'Mr Faber, I'm offering to help you, no strings attached. You've only got to ask. Now where's the problem in that?'

He spoke in the gentlest, most reasonable of tones, but George still felt threatened.

He said, 'There's nothing. Honestly. Nothing I need help with. Please, just go...'

'Nothing?' cried the stranger. 'Your wife's lying dead on the kitchen floor and you're digging her grave in the cellar, and you say there's nothing you need help with? Come on!'

George's eyes orbed in horror and shock. The case was substantially altered!

He stammered. 'Who are you...? Why've you come...? Where have you come from...?'

His mind played blind-man's buff with answers to his questions.

An escaped lunatic? A policeman? Phyllis's lover? But how...? and why...? and what...?

'No, I'm quite sane and I'm not a cop,' interrupted the stranger impatiently. 'Nor am I your wife's fancy man, though incidentally, she did have one, did you know that? Fellow called Freddie who owns the big furnishing store in the High Street.'

'Freddie? You mean Freddie Corcoran?' exclaimed George dumbfounded.

Freddie Corcoran. He thought of him as a friend. They'd got most of their carpets and furnishings from Corcoran's. Freddie had given them an excellent discount...he'd even come round himself to measure up... *Measure up!* The bastard!

But retroactive jealousy was a waste of time. More important was working out how this chap breathing in his face came to know so much...came to be able to read his thoughts even!

'Oh my God,' said George, making perhaps for the first time in his life an imaginative leap. 'You were under the slab, weren't you?'

The young man made no attempt to deny it but smiled and said, 'That's right, Mr Faber. And I can't tell you how grateful I am that you got me out. That's why I want to help you, simply as a token of my gratitude.'

George shook his head, not in denial but for clarity. Good banking practice required that you kept a cool head and dealt solely with facts. He wasn't going to let himself be sidetracked by offers of assistance till he knew precisely what he was dealing with.

'Listen,' he said. 'Who are you? What are you?'

'You can call me Alzac,' said the young man. 'As to what I am, it's a long story and, honestly, I don't really think you want to know. Suffice it to say, I've been shut up down there for rather longer than I care to remember. I was beginning to doubt if I'd ever get out. There was an escape clause, of course, there always is. But as the years rolled by and what you call civilization ground on, it began to look more and more unlikely that it would ever apply.'

'Why?' said George, his ears alert to the whisper of small print. 'What did it say?'

'It said that the stone could only be removed by a priest or priestess who had just made a human sacrifice and still had blood on their hands.'

George looked at his hands. He hadn't noticed the blood till now.

He said, 'I'm not a priest.'

'What do you call yourself then?'

'I'm a banker.'

Alzac smiled.

'That explains it. You're in the service of my old master. I daresay he's got himself a new name now, but back in the old days he was known as Mammon.'

'Mammon? You mean the God of money?'

'Oh no. Hardly a...what you said,' said Alzac. 'But certainly a Power. How shall I explain it to you...? Let me see. Think of it like this. A long time ago when the human race was still finding its feet, often quite literally, the Great Powers decided on a policy of colonization. There were the usual disputes but in the end the distinctive land areas, what you call countries, were carved up and received ambassadors, each according to its own perceived potential.

167

Your country, England, as it came to be known, fell to Mammon. Naturally there was resistance but on the whole things have worked out pretty well, wouldn't you agree?'

'Resistance?' echoed George, unable either to believe or disbelieve what he was hearing. Perhaps he'd had too much beer on top of too much stress...

'Oh yes. The Powers have always had to struggle. How shall I put it? They are on the side of self-determination and market forces, and very much against central control and state interference.'

'You mean, God?'

'You do like that word,' said Alzac frowning. 'But if it helps you understand, yes. In what you call your Middle Ages, Mammon foresaw the huge potential of America and headed west to prepare the ground, leaving me to finish things off here. I got careless. I freely admit it. And I paid the price. I got taken and buried and you lot...' he laughed scornfully '...you lot got art and music and literature, all that stuff you call the Renaissance. It took Mammon a couple of hundred years to regain the lost ground so he didn't waste any effort trying to get me out. He's not what you'd call a forgiving fellow. But clearly he's back on top of things now, which probably explains how I've come to be released. For which I'm enormously grateful. I really owe you a favour. Have you thought of anything yet?'

'Not yet,' said George. 'I'm still thinking.'

As indeed he was, possibly harder than he'd ever thought in the whole of his life. What was happening was quite incredible, of course. But an hour or so ago if anyone had suggested that he was about to murder Phyllis, wouldn't he have found that just as incredible? The difference was, in the latter case there was evidence to convince a reasonable man. A body is a pretty large step in logic. But what test of logical consistency can you apply to something like Alzac?

He said slowly, 'Look, if you are a devil or demon...' (Alzac looked somewhat offended) '...or whatever, why are you so keen to help me? I mean, from what little I know of such things, I never thought your kind went in much for stuff like gratitude?'

Alzac flung his hands apart and shrugged in a gesture which was straight out of a casbah carpet shop.

'Listen, let's forget it,' he said. 'You don't want me to help you, that's OK. No skin off my nose, eh? See if I care.'

The hands came together dismissively and he began to walk away. When he reached the edge of the patio he paused and looked to right and left as if uncertain which way to turn. George watched and waited. Alzac tried a little step left, then a little step right, like a man whose future depended on finding the right direction.

'All right,' said George. 'I've changed my mind. I'd like you to help me.'

His strange visitor spun round, his face lit up with relieved delight as he said, 'That's great. I knew you'd see sense.'

It was the relief that finally convinced George of what he'd begun to suspect.

He pointed a finger triumphantly at the demon or whatever it was and said, 'That does it! I've got your measure, my friend. You're not wanting to help me out of the goodness of your heart, are you? What would a demon's heart be doing with goodness in it anyway? You're doing this because you've got to.'

'What do you mean?' blustered Alzac.

'You know very well what I mean. I bet it's another condition, like the priest and the blood. If someone sets you free, you can't go on your way till you've paid the debt by doing them a favour. I'm right, aren't I?'

For a moment Alzac's fine narrow features began to turn foxy again. Then he recovered and tried a faint smile as he said, 'Aren't you the clever one? All right, Mr Faber, there's an obligation. I don't deny it. So let's get it over with, shall we? Then we can both get back to our proper business.'

'Oh no,' said George. 'I'm not rushing into this. That's what you wanted me to do, wasn't it, you sly bastard? First time you offered to help, if I'd said something flip, like yes, you can close the door as you leave, that would have been it, wouldn't it? Favour done, you completely free. But I reckon this is worth a bit more than that, Mr Alzac. Quite a bit more. Just how far do your powers go anyway?'

'Far enough to turn you into a toad if you don't stop standing there croaking!' snarled the young man.

'Oh yes? And how would I be able to ask you a favour then?' mocked George, feeling very much on top of the game now. 'No, I reckon you can do a lot, a hell of a lot, if you'll pardon the expression. So how about it?'

Alzac's shoulders sagged in defeat.

'All right,' he said. 'You win. I admit it all. And yes, I can do a hell of a lot. I can get rid of your wife's body, for example. No trace. The police can dig and search for a hundred years and they'll never find her. How about that?'

For a second George was tempted.

Then he shook his head.

'No,' he said. 'Getting rid of the body's

not enough. There's still the suspicion, the enquiries...and the guilt. I'm not sure I can live with that.'

Alzac said, 'Well, I'm sorry, guilt's one thing we're not allowed to touch. Tell you what, if you feel so guilty, how about I bring her back to life? That's a real connoisseur's trick, believe me. You'd really be getting value for money there.'

'Back to life?' exclaimed George. 'I'm not sure...back to life...you know, I don't think I really want that either...'

'I wish you'd make up your mind!' cried Alzac. 'This has always been the trouble with you lot. You know what you want, only you can't stand the heat getting it. It's this guilt thing, isn't it? Without that, we'd be masters of the universe by now! All right, here's my final offer. I bring her back to life then I give her a swift heart attack. I know that's really two for the price of one, but what the hell? Today's my rebirthday, I'm feeling generous.'

George was shaking his head.

'No good, I'm afraid,' he said. 'The thing is, I'd still know that it happened because I'd wished it to happen. Are you with me? What I really want is a life without Phyllis, I mean, without her from the start. I was young, I was naïve, I just slipped into marriage before I had enough sense to realise what I was letting myself in for. I don't want to harm her, I just don't want to get tied up with her at an age when neither of us knew any better...'

He paused, took a deep breath, and said, 'That's it. That's what I want. I want to live my life again, but with the knowledge that I've got now from the very start.'

He looked at Alzac expectantly but the demon was shaking his head. 'Sorry, no can do,' he said. 'The trouble is, if you live your life again, your present life won't have happened, and you can't have knowledge of something that doesn't exist, can you?'

George could see the logic of this, but he said desperately, 'All right, let's forget precise knowledge, let's think about... wisdom. That's different, isn't it? The accumulated wisdom of my forty-six years. Couldn't I have that from the start?'

Alzac considered, then nodded slowly.

'Yes, that might be possible, I suppose. You'd live your life again, but be as wise from the start as you are now. That's what you want, is it? You're quite sure?'

'Absolutely,' said George. 'Only...it would be nice to know about it too, about its being a second time around, I mean. But from what you said that wouldn't be possible, would it?'

Alzac looked dubious, then his expression brightened like marsh light on a lonely moor.

'It might be done,' he said. 'But not until you reach the same age you are now. You see, you'll have moved through the same time twice, and it's not until both paths converge at this point of time that you'll be able to see the two of them together.'

'But I'll be able to make a comparison then?'

'Oh yes,' said Alzac.

'Then that's what I want. Definitely. That's the little favour you can do me, my friend.'

'You've got it,' said Alzac. 'Hold tight. Here we go.'

He grinned maliciously, showing more teeth than a human ought to have, raised his left hand, made a circle with his forefinger and thumb, then snapped it open with a fearsome cry.

The air trembled and became full of dust again. George closed his eyes. A current of boiling heat followed by another of crippling cold surged round his veins. He felt the agony of death and the ecstasy of orgasm at the same time.

And then it was past. He felt quite normal again.

He opened his eyes.

He was still standing on the patio with the same flowers in the same tubs, the same black clouds in the same turbulent sky. He was wearing the same clothes. He felt the same twinge of arthritis in his left knee, the same sniffle of headcold in his nostrils.

The only thing different was that Alzac was gone.

My God, he thought, I'm going loopy. Nothing's changed. I've just started having delusions, that's all.

He turned to re-enter the kitchen and stopped in his tracks in the doorway.

Something had changed. Phyllis's body had vanished. There was no sign of it, nor of the Liberty tablecloth, though oddly most of the Tuscan tiles were covered by a large square of carpet.

George looked at his hands. There was no blood on them.

He stepped into the kitchen and looked down at the carpet. No bloodstains here either.

He needed air. He staggered to the door again, his mind struggling to make sense of all these things, or rather to make another sense than that which his powers of logic were printing out as truth.

But truth cannot be denied. He threw back his head and saw it written in the stormy sky.

'Is this it?' he cried in despair. 'Is this all the difference the accumulated wisdom of one lifetime can bring to another? Have

I managed to live through another forty-six years without anything better to show for it than a piece of carpet where there was no carpet before? Oh God. What kind of pathetic excuse for a human being am I?'

There was a rage boiling up inside him which had to be released if it was not to be self-destructive. He let it out on the obvious target.

'Alzac! Where are you? Oh you cunning bastard. You knew, didn't you? You knew I'd do no better second time round and you didn't warn me! Wherever you are, damn you to...to...'

Even in his rage it occurred to him that damning a demon to hell was a touch tautological.

It also occurred to him that perhaps he knew exactly where Alzac was.

He ran into the kitchen, flung open the cellar door and snapped on the switch.

Light flooded down from the unbroken bulb to reveal stone flags, unmarked by pick or shovel, and strewn with household junk.

He began to laugh.

'I didn't kill her second time round so I didn't need to dig up the cellar!' he crowed. 'You're still down there, Alzac. Can you hear me? You're still down there, you stupid bloody demon, and that's where you're going to stay!'

There was a noise something like a groan and he quickly put off the light and slammed the door.

Then he turned and stood on the carpet looking down at the spot where Phyllis's body had lain, and trying to work out whether he was sorry or glad that this time round he hadn't killed her.

But why hadn't he killed her? Could it be perhaps that this time he hadn't wanted to be rid of her? If he'd had a second chance, then she must have had one too. Perhaps she'd made better us of it, suppressing those wilful and domineering elements in her character which made her such a pain to live with. In fact, it came to him in a flash, if he wanted evidence of such a change, he was standing on it!

He recalled her fury when he'd suggested that the way to protect her beautiful tiles from his dirty feet was to put a bit of carpeting down. But this time round she must have given in. And not just a bit of carpet but a large square.

There was something else. The old Phyllis, even if she'd agreed to the carpet, would have chosen a piece of such quality and expense that he probably wouldn't have been allowed to walk on that either! She wouldn't have given house-room to the kind of cheap, rubber-backed nylon-tufted merchandise he was standing on now.

Even the colour was entirely wrong, a garish purple, screaming against the tiles' siennas and the units' olive green. The change this suggested went deeper than simple self-restraint. He racked his brain in an effort to recall what life was like with this new and altered Phyllis.

The new and altered Phyllis, coming up behind him, was pleased to find him so rapt in thought. She buried the hatchet in his skull with one powerful double-handed blow and stood back as he collapsed with scarcely a sound onto the centre of the carpet square specially laid to receive him.

Then she went to the door and softly called, 'Freddie.'

A stocky, gingery man came out of the garden shed. He was pale-faced and his brow was glistening with sweat.

'You've done it?' he said tremulously.

'Of course I've done it,' snapped Phyllis Faber. 'But I can't do everything myself.'

'I'm sorry,' he said as he followed her into the kitchen. 'I don't know what came over me...oh my God.'

Impatiently Phyllis threw a corner of the carpet over George's ruined head.

'Come on,' she said. 'No time to waste. I've got my Age Concern Committee in forty minutes.'

'Look,' said Freddie. 'I've got an idea. Why don't we just bury him in the cellar?

There's a pick-axe in the shed, it'll take no time at all. That'd be best, wouldn't it? A nice grave in the cellar, far less risky...'

His face recovered its colour in a flush of enthusiasm as he went to the open cellar door and peered down into the depths.

But Phyllis was looking at him as if he'd just crawled out of the woodwork.

'For God's sake, Freddie, pull yourself together! That's the most stupid thing I ever heard. We'd need to be brain dead to put him in the first place even our noddy policemen are going to look. Now let's get this carpet folded up and out to your van, shall we?'

'I'm sorry, darling,' said Freddie in a bewildered tone. 'I don't know why...I just got this sudden urge...'

With a perceptible effort of will, he turned his back on the musty darkness of the cellar and came to kneel at her side. Together they folded the carpet over George's body, then bound it round with cord. Next they half dragged, half carried it out of the kitchen, across the patio and round the side of the house to where a furniture van marked *Corcoran's Interiors* stood with its rear doors open and its hydraulic tailboard lowered.

Leaving her lover to manoeuvre the carpet into the van, Phyllis went back into the kitchen and checked the tiles to make sure there was no blood. As she'd anticipated, the rubber-backed carpet had prevented any seepage. Satisfied, she made for the door.

Then she paused. Was that a sound in the cellar?

She went to the open doorway and stood at the top of the steps and listened.

Nothing.

It had probably been a mouse. She shuddered. She was terrified of mice. But she was not a woman who cared to admit such a weakness.

'You just stay down there,' she called. 'Come up here and you'll regret it, believe me!'

Satisfied, she slammed the door shut and hurried out onto the patio.

The storm was just about to break. She didn't see it, but somewhere there must have been a flash of lightning, for as she got into her car and followed the furniture van out of the drive, a peal of thunder rumbled round the circling mountains, like laughter from the belly of a god.

8

Death in Hard Covers
by
MARGARET LEWIS

'Somebody's going to be killed in there, one day,' said the Deputy Librarian cheerfully as he spun the handle and the compact shelving drew itself together like a sea anemone around a shrimp.

'It's quite out of the question, of course! No one could really get trapped.'

He swung the wheel that operated the mechanism and brought twenty feet of metal bookshelves silently together.

'Have a look, Mrs Harper.'

Fay had a look. She did remember something about compact shelving in her own university library, when she was a student. But it wasn't in the well-worn path she had trodden around the English Literature stacks, twenty years ago.

'Well, I think that's all I can show you,' said Angus as they walked up to the issue desk. 'Miss Scott will be your immediate superior, and you'll soon get to know the other girls at the desk. We're a happy bunch here and, of course, you're a Tynesider yourself, aren't you? I'm sure you'll fit in well. Good luck!'

Gazing over his half-moon glasses, Angus Baird was a Thurber original of an absent-minded bookman. Wispy, pale hair curled round his ears like a cherub's. A slight stoop made him seem less tall than he really was. His hands, surprisingly, were muscular and tanned.

'He's not as old as he pretends to be,' thought Fay. 'I wonder why he doesn't smarten himself up a bit.' Her eyes followed him along the catalogues to the offices at the far end. The new library, gleaming with equipment, dominated the northern fringes of the campus. It was a showcase building but with few windows; the atmosphere inside was claustrophobic.

'Right, Mrs Harper.' Miss Scott broke into her thoughts. 'The best way to learn your way around here is to start shelving books. These are all for Level 4—Fine Art, Music and Literature. Just follow the catalogue numbers. This lot should take you about half an hour.' She looked at her watch. 'I'll expect you back at 10.20. Miss James is on duty on that floor if you need help.' She heaved a huge trolley of returned books out from behind the desk and hurried off to answer the 'phone ringing at General Enquiries.

Fay braced herself and set off towards the lift. The trolley, although piled high with heavy books, was easier to manoeuvre than she had expected. By the time she had got in and out of the lift, helped on Level 4 by a rather handsome Arab in well-cut casual clothes, she was almost in control.

'Perhaps this job isn't going to be too bad after all,' she mused. She was lucky to find anything part-time after being a house-person for so long. And she needed the money. Joe's sudden death six months ago had jolted her out of a cosy nest where she never really concerned herself with their financial liabilities. When the solicitor explained to her how little there was to live on, with Sandie and Jennie just starting secondary school, she felt sick with disbelief.

'Self-employed people often postpone their insurance schemes,' kind old Mr Jamieson had said. 'I'm afraid your husband thought that there was plenty of time to make provision for you all.'

Plenty of time! He hadn't even regained consciousness after being hit by a drunken driver. If only the car hadn't broken down that night. If only...

A pleasant Geordie voice startled her out of her thoughts. 'Mrs Harper...Mrs Harper...it is Mrs Harper, isn't it? Can I help you at all?' Fay jumped and realised that she had been wheeling the trolley round and round Level 4 without shelving a single book. She must have passed the Duty Librarian at least twice.

'Oh,' she said, blushing, 'you must be Miss James.'

'Do you realise you've been trundling around here in a kind of trance? Are you ill?'

Fay looked at the tousle-headed girl who had got up from her computer, not much older than her own daughter it seemed.

'No, no, I'm not ill.' She smiled awkwardly. 'This is the first job I've had since the children were born. I haven't quite got back in gear.'

Tousle-hair chuckled.

'What you need is to get that thing *out* of gear and start shelving some books. Come on. I'll point you in the right direction. You don't want the Ancient Artifact up here on your trail, do you?'

'Do you mean Miss Scott?'

'Oh no, she's not so bad. It's Angus Baird, the Deputy Librarian. He's always creeping around making us jump. He thinks it's funny to come up behind you in the stacks and start whispering. He's so bent it's not true. Funny how libraries tend to collect weirdos and nuts, present company excepted, of course.' She grinned at Fay and expertly shelved a handful of music scores. 'Do they come here because they are weird or do they catch it from the atmosphere? Of course the *women* are fairly harmless...'

She rattled on as she walked beside Fay, pointing out the shelving sequences and giving her some useful tips about the most borrowed books and where they were to be found. Fortunately Level 4 was quiet that day, because her summary of the senior staff of the library was far from flattering.

Finally Fay stopped and looked at Di James' cheerful face.

'But if they're so awful, why do you stay? Can't you find another job?'

'Oh, men are all like that. I worked in an office before I took up librarianship. You wouldn't believe the way those managers carried on. Why, in my own section they used to fold up their secretaries' flimsies,'—she peered at Fay quizzically— 'the carbons, you know, and pick them out of the filing basket...a bit of swap and tickle.'

Fay was fascinated. What a sheltered life she had led for years, with the only excitement created by the children's small triumphs in school, and a yearly fortnight's holiday at Whitby or Scarborough.

'There, that's all done. Did she give you a time limit? She usually does for new staff.'

'Oh, lor. Of course she did. I forgot.'
Fay looked at her watch—only five minutes
over time.

'Thanks a lot. I'd never have managed
it without you.'

'That's OK. But you'd better learn to
day-dream and work at the same time if
you want to keep on the right side of the
Mafia downstairs. See you around.'

Di turned back to her abandoned
computer, which was plaintively blinking
with no one taking the slightest notice of
its deep desire to be user-friendly, like a
dog waiting patiently to be taken for a
walk. Fay managed to get through the rest
of the morning without disgracing herself,
and even began to learn the mysteries of
the high-tech issue system. Even so, she
was quite glad to be going home at lunch
time, to tidy up the breakfast wreckage and
to feel empress of her own tiny domain for a
few hours before the children burst in after
school.

Fay had been working happily in the
library for several months before she had to
return any books to the compact shelving
on Level 1, two floors below ground
level.

'Oh, what a nuisance,' said Mrs Scott.
'Those oversized journals will have to go
down to Level 1. You know how to work
the shelving, don't you dear?'

And she bustled off to sort out a rather worried Indian man who was struggling with an Inter-Library Loan Form.

It was very quiet on Level 1 when Fay pushed her trolley out of the lift. This was a popular area during exams; windowless and sepulchral, it cut off the world from desperate students trying to cram three years' work into a few weeks. In fact, thought Fay, with just a vague sense of unease, there's nobody here but me. She paused briefly to admire her new hair style in the control desk mirror. She had had it curled and tousled just like Di James. The children were amazed and then pleased, agreeing that she looked much younger without the rather wispy bun that had been with her far too long. She was wearing trousers for the first time too, like the other girls.

Fay moved down the compact shelving, most of which was closed.

'PER 920,' she mumbled aloud. 'Yes, here we are.'

She twisted the handle and the shelves glided apart. She replaced the periodicals and went on to government papers. Fay was crouched on the floor in the centre of the stack wrestling with a particularly tightly-packed shelf when she heard a slight click in the aisle. She looked up, puzzled, because no one had been around before.

Then, unbelievably, the shelves began to edge together. Petrified, Fay struggled to her feet, shouting 'Look out, I'm in here. Don't close it!'

But the gap was closing, inch by inch. She lunged down the stack, panic-stricken, down the narrowing channel, turning sideways as she went. The shelves were closing tightly around her and she pulled her way along, fighting the increasing pressure and sobbing with terror. Her hands clawed the edge of the shelf and she wrenched her body through into the aisle. The shelves relentlessly continued until the gap was tightly closed.

Fay collapsed on the floor, buttons torn off her blouse, arms cut from the metal rims of the shelves. There was no one there: the aisle was empty. She picked herself up and staggered around to the other side. The faint sigh of the rubber-edged doors met her ears. She ran to the stairs but it was too late. If anyone had been there, they had gone as silently as they came.

Fay made quite an impression on the issue desk when she finally managed to get back upstairs. Shaking uncontrollably, she was calmed down and led off to the staff room, where her story was listened to in amazed silence.

'We must get that system carefully

checked,' said the Librarian, whom Fay had never even said hello to before. 'It must have been a faulty spring. Don't you think so, Angus?'

'Oh definitely, Dr Soames. Since there was no one else there, no other explanation is possible. Is it, Mrs Harper?' He eyed her sharply.

'I—I'm not quite sure. I did think someone was there—but perhaps I imagined it.' Her head was swirling, her arms were aching, she longed to go home. The suggestion of a taxi was gratefully accepted. For some reason, she didn't tell the children what had happened. They might think that someone had tried to murder her! It was all too ridiculous. Fortunately it was the weekend, and by Monday Fay had accepted the rational suggestion that the mechanism had somehow malfunctioned.

'Still, I don't suppose you'll be very keen to go down to the compact shelving again,' said Miss Scott on Monday morning, not entirely unsympathetic. 'But you won't have to. Mr Baird has instructed us that only the librarians are to go into the compact shelving until it has been thoroughly inspected. So just leave anything for there on one side and I'll ask the senior staff to do it some time when we're quiet.'

Upstairs on Level 4, Di James was sitting

making faces at her computer.

' "The Murder in the Library," what?'

'It wasn't funny, Di. I was terrified.'

Di jumped up and pushed the trolley briskly down to the far end. She stopped at the last stack, and turned to look at Fay.

'Actually, I don't think it's funny. And I don't think it was an accident either.'

Fay looked at her in amazement.

'It's not the first accident we've had since this building opened. And, interestingly enough, most of them have been near me.'

'But you weren't anywhere near the compact shelving.'

'I know. But haven't you noticed how alike we are now with your new hair style, and, might I add, your new colour? I think that whoever tightened up the shelves thought I was in there. It's the same person who re-wired my reading lamp in the office a few months before you started. I got a terrific shock but it was such a wet day the roads were like tributaries to the Tyne and I still had my wellies on. What a laugh. The earth wire had been changed around in the plug and the lamp was live. Everyone agreed that it was just an accident then too.'

Di shelved a few books and tidied up a collapsed row.

'And there was something else, too,' she

went on. 'When we were moving from the old site last summer there were piles of books everywhere. Organised chaos. Anyway, for no particular reason, a huge pile fell over on to my desk. I'd just got up to check a reference. Just an accident, of course.'

'But Di, who could possibly want to do this?'

'I've been wondering about it quite a lot. I haven't told anybody up to now and I'm glad I can tell you.'

'Is there anyone who doesn't like you?'

'Lots of people don't like me, but it's a different thing trying to do me in. But look, you'd better get on. Hourly workers must keep busy! I'll see you at coffee—if I survive that long.' She swung off down the aisle to deal with a group of students who were needing advice on projects.

During the break, Di James was busy at the staff notice board renewing her regular feature, MCP of the Week. In a rather naughty frame of very pink pigs and very pink naked men Di had an endless supply of quotations and cartoons that revealed her view of the exploitation of the female by the male. Looking at her aggressive, trouser-clad figure, Fay began to see why Di was not the most popular person in the library.

'Quite a good quote this week,' said Di,

191

coming to sit beside Fay with her mug of black coffee. 'I got it from an industrialist giving a public lecture in Durham last week. Funny how men have these linguistic hang-ups. They just don't have the words right. Do they, Angus?' She lifted her voice as the Deputy Librarian passed by.

His pale eyes rested on her meditatively.

'If you say so, Miss James. You've clearly given the matter a great deal of serious thought.' He looked at Fay. 'Quite recovered, Mrs Harper?'

'Oh yes, it takes more than a scare to stop me,' Fay laughed awkwardly.

'Good, good. That's the way.' He ambled off, the picture of harmless amiability.

'He's a funny bloke.'

'Yes, he is. We've been at daggers drawn for months ever since I found plates missing in the Special Collection he looks after. It was bad enough finding the plates stolen, but even worse when I was the one to discover it. You know, they never found the thief either. I've often wondered if it was someone on the staff, because those books are always kept under lock and key. Very few people actually handle them, and the users were all investigated after the theft. Some of those pictures must be worth thousands—they were birds by Audubon.'

'This place is obviously a hot-bed of crime. And I thought I'd landed a nice peaceful part-time job to keep the wolf from the door.'

'Closed communities always make the best mysteries, don't they?' Di plonked her mug on the counter and departed.

At home that night Fay was curled up on the settee watching a creaky whodunnit on the box and half reading another at the same time. It was hardly surprising that her thoughts turned to the puzzling events at the library that had brought her and Di James together. Was there really a systematic attempt to kill or injure Di? And if so, who was responsible? The person who obviously disliked her most was Angus Baird. But the most likely suspect was never the guilty person, in fiction anyway. That would be far too easy. Still pondering, she drained her hot chocolate and flapped off in her slippers to bed, just checking that there was no undercover activity in the children's rooms. But what, she wondered as she drifted off to sleep, what if Di was imagining all this and hoping to incriminate Angus? What if she deliberately meant to do so? Di was not exactly a straightforward person. Ridiculous, thought Fay as she burrowed under the duvet. I've been reading too many books.

Di James' body was found in the middle of the compact shelving by the cleaners next morning. She had obviously put up quite a struggle, but her rib-cage was cracked and she had literally been crushed to death. The verdict at the inquest was death by misadventure. Investigation of the shelving mechanism showed that the spring closure was improperly adjusted, and the safety stop had failed to function.

Angus Baird left a few months afterwards, promoted to Librarian of East Lancashire University. Fay used to read his poetry occasionally in the Literary Supplement. It was always concerned with bizarre and violent death, particularly of women.

9

Blood Brothers
by
PETER LEWIS

Transcribed and translated from a cassette-recording made surreptitiously by the author in the land of Nod to the east of Eden.

He had it coming to him.

He did.

He really did.

If there's only one thing I'm sure of, it's this.

Believe me.

Believe *me*.

Some hope.

Fat chance. Slim chance. No chance.

I'm wasting my breath, as usual.

But I'm not kidding. No way. Honest.

Certainly not goating. Sorry. I mean gloating.

Slip of the tongue. It's the company *I* keep.

He was the shepherd, remember.

Oh, I know what *you're* thinking, all right. I know exactly what's going on in

195

your mind. You're just like the rest. You've already written me off as a liar and aren't prepared to believe a word I say. I always get the blame. All the blame. Always.

But how could it be otherwise? How could I even begin to compete with the propaganda put out by Big G's PR Department? Fat chance. Slim chance? No chance. If it's written in the Big Old Book, it must be true, mustn't it? And it certainly is written. In black and white. Near the opening so you can't miss it. I can give you the exact reference if you like. Chapter and verse. And not just in words, but Words. WORDS. Supposedly Big G's very own. Supposedly. Do you believe that? You probably do. See what I mean by good PR.

You don't really want to listen to me, do you? At least part of you doesn't. All that righteous part. I can understand that. Highly embarrassing. What will the neighbours say? Even worse, what will they think? To be seen with me, let alone hear me out, is bound to encourage such pernicious gossip about the company you keep. Such dangerous, uncongenial company, eh? Nasty, brutish and—yes—short. By today's standards at any rate. Put it down to the diet. You even act like we're under surveillance. Edgy, nervy. And we may well be. There's a lot of it around in the Middle East. I spy with my little electronic eye, and all that.

I can tell you're more than sorry we bumped into each other in this chance way. Like idly picking a book off a shelf, opening it at random, and getting a nasty shock at what you read. Smut. Dirt. Filth. You may not find it easy to put the book down, but you'd much rather be off, vamoose, make a quick exit, would you? You wouldn't want to be observed with something like that in your hands.

Don't think I'm blaming you. Not at all. In your shoes I'd be the same. After all, I am, by *all* accounts, the villain of the piece. Supposed to be the original deep-dyed villain. Ur-villain, if you know what that means. The person who gave killing a bad name. The founding father of violent death. The inventor of murder. Or should it be discoverer? Either way, the first of many. Very, very many. The rot started with me. That's the official story.

So in the eyes of the world, I'm guilty without question. Incidentally, guilty without trial, defence counsel, or any of the legal procedures that even the People's Courts in the Third Reich felt it necessary to employ, in a manner of speaking. Even a show trial or a kangaroo court might be better than no trial, no court. Might. I'd like to have heard what the victims of Stalin's purges had to say about that. But I'm just guilty. Plain guilty. Guilty by divine diktat, and sentenced to be a vagrant and a wanderer. No questions asked. No need to ask questions. No need for evidence, even. And certainly no right of appeal. On what grounds, for heaven's sake? When justice is dispensed from on high, how could anyone have any doubts? Fat chance. No chance. That would be heresy. Apostasy. That would require imagination.

Have you noticed that people are forever going on about how imaginative they are, and poets with inward eyes and lakeland mud on their boots about how wonderful the human imagination is? A gift of Big G, or some such cliché. The sublime! Subliminal, more like. You must know all about it, coming from Cumbria. Poets tripping over themselves to reach the top of Helvellyn or some equally Big G-forsaken summit in order to commune with—what? Thin air? Wet sheep? There can't be much else up there. At least here *his* sheep were dry. Then there's all that cant about consciousness raising, expanding awareness, and reawakening subconscious powers. But what I want to know is this. If there's all this wonderful imagination pouring out of everyone's ears, and everybody's being raised, expanded and reawakened, why is it that someone somewhere sometime hasn't said:

Now hang on. Wait a minute. Is this the way it happened? Can we be certain of this? Where's the unquestionable evidence? Where's the evidence? Isn't it possible that there is another version of events? Couldn't there be another side to this story? Who's telling it anyway, and how do we know it isn't biased, distorted, inaccurate, or even downright false? After all, rewriting history is as old as the hills—well perhaps not that old, let's say as old as Dad—I mean Adam—so how do we know that this hasn't been rewritten? Are we dealing with a reliable narrator? And even if we are, how reliable is he? Some tale teller said, "Trust the tale, not the teller," but should we trust either? Let's face it, "telling tales" means "fibbing" or "lying", doesn't it?

I'll give you an example. Chapter and verse. In black and white. What a pedant would call a textual crux. No, don't get excited. Textual, I said. Textual. Not a slip of the tongue. You know the bit, the famous bit, in which I'm alleged to ask a question about being my brother's keeper. Everybody knows that, so it must be true, mustn't it? But is it what I really said? Like a nanny goat's left testicle, it is. So how do you explain that? Go on. Try.

Either I'm the victim of systematic

disinformation and there's a helluva cover-up scam going on. Or Big G's hearing wasn't too good that day. Wax in His ears, or tinnitus, or something. He's not perfect. You don't have to read all those post-this and post-that French philosophers who specialise in slips of the word, slips of the tongue, to know that there's something decidedly dodgy about the concept of omniscience. Anyone who knows Him at first hand can vouch for the fact that He's not all He's cracked up to be. As I mentioned before, He relies on great PR. The angelic host. Best image-makers going. Best intelligence gatherers, too. Knock the CIA into a hocked cat. Sorry, *that* was a slip of the tongue. What chance does a solitary individual have against an organisation that big?

I suppose you're curious to know what I really said—if I said anything. But would you believe me if I told you? Fat chance. Slim chance. No chance. Have three guesses. Go on. But it wasn't "Who's got my brother's kipper?" or "Is my brother a copper?" or even "Has my brother come a cropper?" You look very puzzled. No idea? Give up? Well I'm not letting on at the moment. I've learned the hard way that everything you say—even if you don't say it—is taken down, altered and used in evidence against you.

Take that phrase I just used about Big G: "cracked up to be". I know you're not supposed to question His omninesses, but I wasn't being gratuitously insulting. It's simply that no one can be that omni in a rapidly expanding universe full of black holes, blue moons, quarks, quasars, and Big G knows what. Only He doesn't. That's the point. But imagine what a tabloid journalist would do to my words if you let him loose on them for ten seconds. You can see the headlines:

**Fratricidal psychopath accuses
Big G of being cracked**

Or:

**Big G off his rocker, according
to warped killer**

"What is truth?" asked that Roman ponce in the Small New Book. But he didn't stay for an answer because he damn well knew there was no answer. The questions you have to ask are: "Whose truth? Which truth?" You don't have to read Michel Foucault—although it helps—and I am trying, honest—to know that truth, like power, comes out of the barrel of a gun. Those in authority decide. Sometimes it's been priests. Sometimes

201

kings. Sometimes queens—let's not forget the fair sex can be as ruthless, cruel and unscrupulous as us. Sometimes theologians. Sometimes lawyers. Sometimes politicians. Sometimes scientists. But they're all the same. Dictators. Oligarchic dictators. Fascist dictators. Communist dictators. And the slyest, foxiest of them all, democratic dictators.

Sometimes I really wish Big G were omnipotent and would zap, zap, zap, zap, zap like He did in the Big Old Book. The world could do with a good zapping. But He went soft in the Small New Book. Mercy, forgiveness, love, reconciliation—all that kind of malarkey. Yet it has to be said in His defence that there's been far more bad zapping than good zapping. So often it's the wrong guys who get zapped. Examples are endless. Passchendaele, Treblinka, Dresden, Hiroshima.

Any thoughts on the matter? I didn't think so. Too much to hope for. So what's keeping you? Curiosity? You want to see if I've still got blood on my hands, is that it? Well have a good look. Go on. Don't be squeamish. Spotless, aren't they? Not a speck. Are you waiting for me to say something about a little water cleansing me from some crime or other? Fat chance. I'll leave that to the Scots. Hypocrites.

Yet remember that Mac the Knife and his wife are made out to be tragic. Yes, great tragic figures. They move people to tears. They butcher a saintly old man, frame his servants before liquidating them, hire hitmen to waste an old buddy of Mac's—and that's just for starters—and still move people to tears. Can you believe it? What's going on here? How's it done? What's the trick? It's obviously OK to be *tragic*. Some people can kill to their heart's content and still be tragic. After bopping off his pop, Oedipus married his mum—and what do you know? He's *tragic*. Not a dry eye in sight, even though his sight wasn't too good by the end. The Greeks really could get away with murder. Beats me. Is it something to do with race? Given what I've been through, I'm the one who ought to be tragic, but I'll wait a very long time for someone to call me that. Someday, perhaps? Fat chance. Slim chance. No chance. If I put out my eyes in an attempt to win sympathy, everyone would laugh. Big joke.

You almost make me feel I should apologise for my clean hands. Must be disappointing for you. If you want to see red, I can recommend the medieval Mystery Play about me and—him—because the actor representing me puts on red gloves. That's the best I can offer. You can pick it up at the York Festival. So what else are you hoping I'll produce? Gruesome photographs of the victim? The alleged weapon? The statement by the scene-of-the crime investigators? The pathologist's report? The forensic evidence? An amateur video surreptitiously taken by the Angel Gabriel as a snuff movie to entertain Big G? You may be playing with fire and brimstone here. Curiosity killed the cat, remember, and there's nothing like killing to excite curiosity.

How would the theatre have survived without it? Or cinema? Or TV? Why were public executions so enormously popular for toffs and proles alike? Nothing like a good hanging, drawing and quartering—drop, top, chop, lop—to pull the crowds in. Pull in the crowds, it should be. I know. Never end a sentence with a preposition, my schoolmaster used to yell as he laid into me with his ca— —let's call it his rod—but I never caught on. Unlike *him*. Young clever clogs. By the way, should that be, "but on I never caught"?

Yes, death in the afternoon has always been good business—not only in the corridas of Spain. Lions and Christians. Thumbed-down gladiators. Heads in nooses. Heads on spikes. Heads in baskets. Slice, slice, slice. Breaking on the wheel. Bash, smash, crash. Burning at the stake. Sizzle,

sizzle, sizzle. Tearing apart with red-hot pincers. Snip, clip, rip. Pulling apart with four wild horses. Snap, crack, pop. A really good stretch—even better than a crucifixion. Now that was a death in the afternoon to remember. You name it. We do it. What it's all about is meeting a need, catering for public taste. Bums on seats, to use the jargon of mass entertainers, although much more often it's standing room only, except for the toffs on their grandstand balconies.

We may not like to admit it, even to ourselves, but we're all voyeurs, glued to the small screen for the next newscast about war, mayhem, carnage, catastrophes, slaughter, and terrorist atrocities. And, as the saying goes, there's nothing like a good murder. Fact or fiction, murder sells better than hot cakes. Perhaps that's not a good comparison, come to think of it. How often do you see *them* for sale?

Poets, it is said, are often half in love with death, but most of us are less scrupulous and go the whole hog—as long as it's somebody else's. Whenever there's a plane crash somewhere not totally inaccessible, the souvenir hunters are out like locusts hoping for ghoulish momentoes. Call in police frogmen to retrieve the corpses of drowned boaters or swimmers from a lake or river and you're sure of a highly attentive audience. No sooner has a murder been committed than the weapon is a collector's item.

Since you're still with me, so far, I have to conclude that like the Ancient Mariner I exert a certain fascination. But he was guilty, remember. He confessed to everything. At least according to that poet with lakeland mud on his boots he did. No, not Daffodil Will. The other one. The one whose name begins with C, like mine. Why is it people find notoriety much more seductive than honourable fame? But the last thing I want to do is trade on my notoriety. I'm trying to clear my name. Get the case reopened. Have the verdict quashed. Put the record straight. Win compensation for wrongful arrest, wrongful conviction, wrongful sentence, wrongful everything. I know. Fat chance. Slim chance. No chance. What chance at all when it is indelibly fixed in the Big Old Book in Words. WORDS.

At one time I was going to change my name by deed poll in the hope of making a new start. After all, even Big G did that—a *good* precedent if ever there was. He wasn't always Big G, remember. In the Big Old Book He's Yahweh or YHWH or Jahweh or JHWH or Yahveh or YHVH or Jahveh or JHVH or even Jehovah. Myself I must remake, I thought, although a poet with Irish mud on his boots is always given credit for that much-quoted phrase. Plagiarist. Go west, young man, I told myself. Try somewhere less noddy to the west of Eden for a change. But there was the problem of the mark Big G had put on me after the contretemps. That was a really mean trick since it was a complete giveaway and couldn't be disguised. I might as well have had neon lights across my chest spelling out my name.

I wasted a lot of money on over-priced women's cosmetics from department stores, looking for a magic potion. Some super-foundation cream or other. No luck. I asked about plastic surgery on the health service, but you can imagine what the waiting lists are like. You'd wait eons. As for the private sector. Fat chance. Slim chance. No chance. For a mere tiller of the soil like me, the prices sounded like the distance of stars measured in kilometres rather than light years. In any case Big G wasn't pleased when He found out what I was thinking of. There's another of my prepositional solecisms. Do you know what my favourite sentence is? That's something I'd rather do something else than. Made my schoolmaster reach for his riding crop, that did.

Do you know what Big G said when He found out? He warned me that if

I got rid of the mark by hook or by crook—that may have been a reference to the people who run private health care, but I'm not sure—you can never tell with Big G because He's so tricksy with words, Words, WORDS—He may have been alluding to a bishop—anyway if I did get rid of it He'd immediately provide me with another one, or two for good measure. *Good* was His word—I mean Word. Was He being ironic about retribution? Perhaps. Or perhaps it's just that all the forgiveness and reconciliation that arrived with the Small New Book doesn't apply retrospectively to people like me.

Suffering was necessary for my spiritual development, Big G explained, for redemption, for salvation, and He lent me a really tacky copy of *Pilgrim's Progress,* full of coffee stains and bits of squashed food, to further *my* progress. Yuck. Precious first edition it may have been, but yuck. That argument never cut much ice with me, but in this climate, as you've noticed, it's difficult to get ice to cut in the first place. I nearly told Him that I'd gladly give up the suffering even if it meant I couldn't be redeemed or saved, but I thought better of it. Remember, I knew Him before He was into the mercy and love of the Small New Book, and half-expect Him to revert at any moment to the inveterate zapper of old.

When He first put the mark on me, I pleaded with Him to finish me off instead. Zap me, I screamed, just zap me. I can't go around like this. Crucify me, or something. And do you know what He said? Now that is an interesting suggestion—His very Words. And He got out His little notebook and jotted something down. That might come in useful, He added, but it's too good for the likes of you. Notice, yet another *good*. It's always on the tip of His tongue. And His tongue doesn't slip. At one time He liked to be called Good G rather than Big G, but became upset when, I quote, the alliteration led to a systematic abuse of its exclamatory potential—or some such high-falutin phrase of the kind He goes in for. Two prepositions there. I'm excelling myself today.

He's always been heavily into marks and signs, icons and symbols. Rainbows, floods, burning bushes, stars. You name it. He does it. Semiotics, He calls it. Semi-idiotics, more like. He was going to lend me another book to help me understand marks and their multiple meanings—some yank fairytale called *The Scarlet Letter*, which sounded to me like the latest in coloured and flavoured condoms. You can see the way my mind runs. But when He said something about Puritans, I declined politely, made some dubious doctrinal excuse. *Pilgrim's Progress* was more than enough for me. I don't mind reading. I like a good book. Repeat, *a* good book. I didn't say, *the* good book. But I like to see words on the page, not the breakfasts of messy eaters, however high-minded and Non-conformist and sanctimonious and Presbyterian they are.

According to Big G, marks can now be a sign of grace, not a punishment. Apparently there have been people who welcome certain marks and were proud of them. Stigmata, especially. Not that *they* were ever on offer to me. I'm supposed to have more than enough blood on my hands as it is. I grant you that there have been lots of changes since the Small New Book, but I was born too soon, far too soon to be born again. The only marks Big G dispensed when I was young were black ones, and I can't think of mine as anything but a curse. Yet He's always urging me to think positively, make the best of things.

Abandon all this existentialist nausea and nihilism you've been wallowing in for years, He says. That went out with the flood—speaking metaphorically, of course. It's now as passé as the missionary position, He insists. Time to join in all the jolly postmodernist fun and games. Go ludic. Be playful. Swim in a sea of floating signifiers.

(Believe it or not, this is how He talks nowadays.) Alter your parameters. Interface with the other. Expand your consciousness. Raise...

Even Big G caught His breath at that point. You can guess why. My name has uncomfortable associations with that word. Why me? Why pick on my name? Couldn't the phrase be, raise Lazarus? Maybe not. Too ambiguous. Or, raise Dick? Same problem. Why does language have to be so ambiguous it's almost unusable? OK, let's try raise Calvin. Only marginally different from my name and much more appropriate. I really feel incensed about the liberties people have taken with my name—and my life story. Misspelling it. Getting it wrong. Using it to frighten the children. One of the worst examples was that forties movie you must have seen since everybody's seen it. Supposed to be one of the greatest films ever made, if not the greatest. The one in which I'm labelled Citizen as though I'm something out of the French Revolution. Sounds better in French, doesn't it? *Citoyen*. Anyway I couldn't recognise myself in that, at all. No resemblance whatsoever. A complete travesty.

As you might expect, I wasn't even consulted. Not as much as a by-your-leave, let alone a credit. They just borrowed my name to ensure a good box-office. What really got my goat—that reminds me, I must milk that transsexual nanny—was the very end, if you remember, when this deep booming voice, like Big G rehearsing His announcement of the Last Judgment, declares: My name is Orson Welles. Why did he leave it so late? Why didn't he say so at the beginning instead of pretending that he's me all the way through?

I sometimes think Plato was right about poets and artists and writers. Send the whole pack of them packing. You'd notice the difference in your part of the world—had more than your fair share. What a collection! Fibbing, lying, telling tales. Making a song and dance about Poetic Truth as though it were the nearest thing to Big G's Word. Or even better. They are becoming the priests of your time. The new clericalism. But they're just as full of windy preaching and their own farty importance as the old lot. Ordering everyone to be pluralistic. The tyranny of aesthetes could be worse than that of the politically correct. Unacknowledged legislators of mankind, my less deceived arse. Who needs legislators, acknowledged or otherwise? All they do, like your mum and dad, is fuck you up.

Hollywood's got a lot to answer for. Not only that Citizen thing. I could go on all day about what they've done to the Big Old Book—and the Small New One, come to that—but just one more example. Promise. Do you remember Jimmy Dean? Came to a squishy-squashy end in a car crash. Zapped by his own Porsche. Cult hero, all right. Rebel without a cause. Opposite of me because I've got causes to spare. The movie I'm thinking of—try again—of which I'm thinking—is *East of Eden*. A title to conjure with, my friend, because that's where we're standing. This is the place. All around us. Take a really good look. Did the film appear remotely like this? The only thing *it* was east of was the Pacific Ocean. I've been around a bit and I can recognise Southern California when I see it. Another big con. And as for telling my story... And they got my name wrong—again. On purpose, you think, to avoid paying my copyright fee.

How can the media whizsetters and jetkids get away with it? Slipped again there, didn't I? How do they succeed in fooling all of the people all of the time? Zapping's too good for the likes of them. I nearly sued this time. I'd had enough. But have you any idea what a yank lawyer costs? Doctors and lawyers must split the entire GNP between them. Talk about division of the spoils.

As you've noticed I'm very touchy about

my name. From the first it seemed odd that I, the first born, should be given a name beginning with the third letter, C, whereas *he*, the second born, had one beginning with A, just like Dad. It was as though he were getting a higher exam grade than me. Alphabetically both of us were ahead of Mum, of course, which is how things used to be in days of patriarchal yore. Now don't get me wrong. I'm not defending primogeniture, male hegemony, gender hierarchies and the absence of women priests in your English Church. Someone my age could hardly claim to be a new man, but I'm all for equal opportunity—women tilling the soil for a change—*and* I've been brainwashed by the anti-Freudian fems into clitina-envy. Or is it vagoris-envy? I can never remember.

Another thing bothered me about our names. His name was full of positive connotations. It suggested competence, talent, skill, efficiency, resourcefulness, ability. Mum and Dad even nicknamed him Seaman. My name, on the other hand, had much darker associations; punishment, pain, six of the best, stripped and striped bottoms. What's in a name, you may ask. Perhaps your entire destiny. I've certainly had my fill of punishment and pain. And I also had a naval nickname, but note the difference: Mutineer. A joky reference, I gather, to a bestselling war story about an American destroyer with some version or other of my name. Predictably enough, Hollywood made a film version with another cult hero, Humphrey Bogart. Anything connected with my name seems to make money for them.

Mutineer may have been joky, but wasn't it inviting trouble? Especially linked with Destroyer. Words create expectations, perhaps even realities. Were Mum and Dad trying to turn me into a rebel? Were they conditioning me to jump over Big G's traces, kick against His pricks, perhaps to get back at Him after that fruit-picking foul-up in Eden? It's a theory, a conspiracy theory, but in my view they just weren't thinking. Another almighty cock-up—one of theirs, I mean, not the Almighty's—like falling for that serpent's cock-and-apple story. Anyone else would have realised it was a load of bull. But back in those pre-SNAFU days—prelapsarian's the posh word—there wasn't anyone else. They were innocents at heart, unworldly people, and since names and nicknames were so new, Mum and Dad didn't realise the effect they can have. Understandable in the circumstances. Much less so today. Yet you still come across kids called John Thomas and Willy Long. The parents some children have.

215

If I *was* disadvantaged, it wasn't intentional, but there's no doubt that a number of things were tilted in Seaman's favour. And he was the favourite, all right. He was the pet. Mr Clean-Squeaky. There I go again. Mr Nice Guy. It wasn't that I was prodigal or anything. In the days of the Big Old Book, prodigal sons were more likely to be zapped than fed the fatted calf. Wienerschnitzels with all the trimmings for penitent ne'er-do-wells came much later. Big G had to alter His parameters, interface with the other, change His name by deed poll, and do a bit of incarnating before switching to universal compassion.

No, I was just too tired after labouring all day in the fields of our kibbutz to turn on the charm and the wit the way Seaman could. I was the one who had to grind away at the soil: plough, till, hoe, sow, harvest. He had it easy, swanning around with his flock, tootling on his baroque flute, imagining he was an Arcadian shepherd in some Golden Age pastoral frolic cooked up at Versailles by Marie Antoinette in her phony milkmaid's rig, while the sans-culottes were reduced to eating Black Forest Gateau or something equally unhealthy and saturated with cholesterol. No wonder her head ended up in the basket.

Obviously I didn't like him very much.

I admit I was envious. I wasn't desolate when he snuffed it. I could contain my grief with some ease. I didn't cry my eyes out at the Requiem Mass. Sat back instead and enjoyed the music. I don't trust angels as far as I can throw them—getting hold of them in the first place is the problem—but they do sing divinely. In some ways Seaman was asking for it. He had it coming to him. But that doesn't mean I killed him. If we killed everyone we didn't like or felt envious of, the human race would be extinct in less time than it takes a Greenpeace activist to find evidence of environmental pollution or the World Wildlife Fund to locate another endangered species.

What bugged me was that he was so two-faced. Proper little Janus. Nice as pie, Mum and Dad would say of him. And he was—on the surface. There's no denying it. But when people use that phrase, I always remember a Black Civil Rights leader in the States commenting that violence was as American as cherry pie. After that, pies lost their innocence for me. I imagined them biting me back or blowing up in my face. They might look delectable with fluffy pastry on top, but how could you be sure of what was underneath? What if it turned out to be sloeberries? Or toadstools? I don't want to make a meal of this, but believe me, there was much more to Seaman than sugar and spice and all things nice.

Whatever it was, I suggest you put it down to Original Sin. But remember, Original Sin was hot off the press at the time, and we were only just beginning to explore its possibilities. Seaman, I suspect, was ahead of the game—the avant-garde. The last straw for me was when he pulled a fast one by pulling out all the stops to pull the wool over Big G's eyes. The version in the Big Old Book bears as much resemblance to the truth as—what was that phrase Mum coined?—as a hawk to a handsaw. It's the bit about presenting offerings to Big G. I arrived quietly with some produce of the soil, but he made an entry like a presidential candidate at a Republican Party convention with choreography by Martha Graham. Talk about showbiz, razzmatazz. Dressed up to the nines, he was, in freshly cut vines. You half-expected drum majorettes on the backs of elephants, doing high kicks and flashing their knickers.

I didn't know what to say. Words failed me—unlike Big G, Who's never lost for them. Yet He fell for it. Surprisingly gullible. It made me wonder whether Mum and Dad were doing no more than imitating Him when *they* fell. By the time Seaman handed over the tastiest-looking members of his flock, together with a bowl of freshly made mint sauce, Big G was cock-a-hoop and turning cartwheels. I know He's partial to lamb chops, but to be taken in so easily. So now you know why Big G turned His nose up at my humble fare, as the Big Old Book implies. I think that's enough about *him*. One shouldn't speak ill of the dead—however duplicitous.

There's not much more to say. I assume you're hanging on in the hope I'll make some sensational disclosure about whodunnit. Not that you'll believe me. Fat chance. But there's no disguising that somebody dunnit. One glance at the corpse was enough to rule out accident or suicide. Nothing self-inflicted about that wound. No sirree, as they say in Hollywood movies. I considered the possibility of one of the animals, since some of them had got a bit out of hand since leaving the Garden, but that made no sense. He'd been struck down in one fell swoop, whatever that is, not bitten, chewed or mauled. For a while I couldn't bring myself to think it, but eventually I had to. Could it have been Mum? Dad? Mum and Dad? But why? They doted on him. Anyway they did have a perfect alibi, confirmed by cherubim. There were more of them around in those days, before we had spy satellites. They'd spent the day among the fig trees, making new clothes—and, by the look of exhaustion on their faces, playing that new outdoor game of Lady Chatterley and Mellors they'd read about in *Woodland Pursuits*.

If they were in the clear, it didn't require the ratiocinative power of Sherlock or Hercule or another of those cerebrally grey men to work out the mathematical consequences. If there were only three of us around, and two weren't anywhere near where the action had been, that left—yours truly. Logic had me over a barrel. It *had* to be me. Yet it wasn't. That was the moment when I recognised that rationalism is totally irrational. One man's rationality is another man's hocus-pocus. But the mind can play tricks on us. Could I have done it, I asked myself, without knowing what I was doing and without remembering a thing about it? In a trance? Under hypnosis? And when Big G Himself began to accuse me, I almost convinced myself that this was the explanation. But in my heart of hearts, wherever that's located, I was uneasy. There had to be another solution. And it took me ages—I mean ages—to find it.

What gave me the clue was watching TV programmes about military exercises that went horribly wrong. Like the hundreds of

American GIs who copped it accidentally in the English Channel during the preparations for D-Day. Or the British soldiers who were irradiated during nuclear tests in Australia. The type of mistake quickly concealed by Official Secrets Acts, fifty-year prohibitions on sensitive documents, and any other legislative manoeuvre to hand.

Anyway that's how I twigged it. Seaman had been zapped—by accident. I was speculating, admittedly, relying on guesswork, but it was the only theory that held water. After Original Sin came on the agenda, Big G was obviously going to need some type of secret weapon as a last resort, and He presumably handed the Zapper project over to the more technological of the angelic host—those who had solved the equations relating to dancing on the point of a pin. Seraphim, they were—the boffins of their age. They won't admit it—*they* never do, do *they?*—but one of the test firings must have gone badly wrong.

They must have aimed the prototype Zapper at one of the sheep—experiments on live creatures have a much longer history than even Animal Rights activists realise—but hit Seaman instead. My guess is that they were trying to be too clever by half and were trying to kill two birds with one stone. Doubly ingratiate themselves with Big G by providing barbecued lamb as evidence of their successful development of the Zapper. Instead they'd ballsed it up. Good and proper. Right, left and centre. So they needed a goatscape pronto. Sorry, you know what I mean. And there I was. I bet all hell broke loose when Big G found out about Seaman—the seraphim responsible may even have been despatched *there* to do a bit of bird—but He wasn't going to broadcast the truth, was He? How could He and keep His image intact? Who would have believed in all His alleged omninesses? He'd have given the show away during the opening bars of the overture if He hadn't gone along with the frame-up. All that was needed to make it holy writ was to publish it in the Big Old Book. QED. Bob's your uncle. I didn't have a chance. I didn't have any uncles, either. Couldn't have. Mum and Dad were only children, remember.

But I haven't given up hope. While there's life, there's hope. Some hope. Unless you've actually been zapped, it's always worth trying to rectify miscarriages of justice. Since you've been so patient with me, I'll let you into a secret. Top secret. Cross your heart and hope to be zapped. What gives me hope is that I've ben able to hack into Big G's archive, right back to the earliest records. Before the Big Bang. Wow! I'm not going to start on that now—I've taken enough of your time—but, Wow! You've no idea. The Astronomer Royal from some high-security-prison city up your way—Durram, I think, somewhere to do with sheep anyway—is on the phone or fax every day. The Big Old Book's going to need rewriting from top to bottom and from back to front. "In the beginning," it begins, but there was no beginning, so how's the revised version going to begin?

What I did was finally work out His computer password. Worse than cracking Enigma. And anyone who wants it is going to have to pay through the ears, nose and throat for it—and all the other orifices as well. I'm slowly piecing together the evidence—it's still circumstantial—but it's going to knock the Dead Sea Scrolls into a—last time I tried to say it I got in wrong—hacked cot. Would you believe it? Hot cack. My brain's giving out. Need a siesta. I know I'll be called a forger and a faker and a fantasist and a paranoid geriatric. But for the first time I'm in with a chance. Fat chance? Slim chance? But better than no chance. When you think about it, there was always something wrong with the idea that the most likely suspect dunnit. That's against the rules. You'll have to excuse me now, I'm about to collapse. But help yourself to some fruit. The apples are delicious. You'll have to pick your own, I'm afraid. Watch out for the s...sszz.

Forget what it means. It means ten grand's worth of debt written off for a delivery job. So just go where it leads you and don't ask why.

The address on the back of the old betting slip was a back-street curry house in Bradford. The fat Pakistani waiter telephoned and said it'd be half an hour. Dave had just spooned up the last of a greasy chicken korma with a chapati and was sketching the waiter on a paper napkin when a dapper, light-skinned Asian sat down opposite him. Couldn't be more than twenty-two, twenty-three. Greased-back hair and distrustful eyes.

'Mr Malik? Jonah sent me. Dave.'

He wiped his hand on the sketch of the waiter and offered to shake. Malik stared at Dave's stubby fingers doubtfully; raised his own right hand to summon the fat guy and demanded something in Urdu. 'You write nothing down. You have to memorise a place and time in Amsterdam and a phone number in Leeds. Think you can manage that?'

His accent was a mixture of Yorkshire and Asian; his tone was scornful. *Think you can manage that?* Dave's memory contained without difficulty how many pints every customer had ordered every day of the week—plus which of them would know their order so he'd remember not to overcharge them. He nodded, curtly. Malik gave him the place and time and phone number. A glass of water arrived with ice and a slice of lemon and several globules of grease floating in it. The Asian drank it down in one gulp while Dave asked what it was he was delivering.

'Use your imagination,' said Malik, wiping his mouth with a white hand-kerchief. 'If you have one. Whatever you do, though: don't go opening it, will you now? The package. Bye.'

Malik turned to talk to the waiter at the back of the room. Dave's fingernails dug into his hands, beneath the table. It was only when he was halfway down the street, punching his right fist hard into his left palm, that he realised he hadn't paid for the curry. Sod it. Sod them. Charge it to Jonah.

Another bar; another rope round his neck. He wanted to tell Siggy about the job and Jonah saying not to call him Dada and how he thought Pauline must have been talking to Jonah's wife for his dada to turn against him like that. But Siggy was having one of her cantankerous days and only wanted to rail at him about why he wouldn't come and live with her. 'You know how much I want to but I can't, I just can't. Everything's in Pauline's name 'cause of the taxman: you know that. I can't, like I can't even buy a condom without her knowing about it.'

'You make a joke of everything, you. But not of me, you do not.'

'For God's sake, Siggy...'

'I tell you, Da-vid...'

She had a way of saying his name—as if it were two words, with an angry bite of her lower lip on the "v"—that still made him tremble, still made him want to touch her cheek softly while he replied, in gentle parody, "Sig-run". Not now, though. No. Not when all she had to say was...

'No,' she was insisting. 'No more...'

But he was already on his way to the bar. What did she know? You could see from her eyes she'd already had more than her first joint of the day. Dope-head. No woman was going to tell Da-vid what to do.

Actually, they were always telling him what to do. And he always thought about obeying. None of them, though, had found a way to stop him drinking the next drink. He added a whisky chaser to the order. Not for the pleasure of it. He knew some people enjoyed drinking—look at them all, sipping their spritzers and Mexican beers (poncy bloody places she dragged him to)—but he'd lost the knack of it somewhere along the line. Probably when he and Pauline were running their own place and he and his mates had drunk away the profits and were just getting stuck into the losses. That was when the urge for the next had got stronger and the reason for the urge had become more and more mysterious.

Like sex, he imagined joking wryly to Siggy, saving it up for the post-coital scene later, once he'd promised to leave Pauline again and the hard look in her eyes had melted with his easy lies and the next couple of joints. You know, Sig, he'd say—stroking the soft skin under the jut of her jaw, kissing her bony shoulder—I mean, why am I here? I've got the urge but I don't know the reason. And her hand would be in his hair...

The corner table was empty. She'd gone. 'Cunt,' he meant only to think but heard himself saying, his hands suddenly trembling, the carefully-balanced beer splashing into his scotch and her vodka. 'Ess,' he added to the posh woman with the sneer on the next table, 'she's Swedish y'know, titled, it's just the way she says it: Cuntess.'

Blather blather blather. *You make a joke of everything, you.* He loved the way she shouted at him, took no bullshit, stormed out of pubs. Yes he did. Usually. It's just that today, today, my God I'm definitely not going to cry, today, please...

He sat down at the table, his outstretched hands still clutching the three drinks, and watched tears drip, two by two, on to the scratched wood.

'Just for a couple o' days.'

'With her, I don't doubt.' Prim, like her mother, Pauline could be.

'Polly, I told you, it's all over with her...'

'You're a terrible liar.'

'That's why I always tell you the truth.'

He smiled. She reached for another licorice allsort. Her teeth were blackened with them. He couldn't stop looking at her mouth, chewing. He shrugged. That was all he could do with Pauline these days: smile and shrug. She was ironing. The kids' tee-shirts lay there, their creases relentlessly effaced. Another licorice allsort. That's all you do, eat.

He never said things like that to her any more. He smiled again. 'So I'll be back Thursday.'

She was smoothing out one of his white hankies with the D laced in the corner in fancy lettering. Happy Christmas Dad. David wiped his mouth. 'And aren't you going to tell me? Where you and your fancy piece are off to?'

'Polly, it's not like that.'

'Meaning, you aren't going to tell me?'

'Meaning...'

He shook his head and just walked away to pack his bag. It's better that you don't know. There are worse things than fancy pieces. And it is a far far worse thing that I do than I have ever...

He'd booked a cabin on the Rotterdam ferry—nothing but the best, from the milk profits fund he didn't even tell Siggy about—but he couldn't sleep. So he prowled the corridors and decks, inspecting the plan of the ship for lifeboats and talking to the Siggy in his head, the one who forgave him, the one who understood. Not the one who left the answerphone on when he was sure she was in. Not the one who didn't answer the doorbell when the lights were on in her flat.

Use your imagination. A group of laughing people—a tall blonde woman in her thirties and a group of anonymous men—seemed to stop laughing at his approach. He thought he heard one of the men mutter his name.

He wished he'd brought his sketch-pad with him. Something to make him imagine better. Something to stop him conjuring up forgiving Siggys and kindly Dadas and strangers who are using your name in

232

conversation. Have another drink. Ten grand for a parcel. Don't think about it, don't think about it.

You see, he said, sitting on the pavement outside the railway station in Amsterdam, amid American back-packers and the clank and clack of the trams, you see, Sig, I need other people. Like I said to you that time when you looked at my stuff: I can't do self-portraits. When I'm on my own I kind of, vanish. This is the sum total of what I am: a delivery man. If I don't pass messages to and fro I disappear. Mercury, messenger of the gods, sort of thing.

Ten thousand quid to pick up a package in Amsterdam and deliver it to someone in Leeds. What bloody gods were these?

Find a bar. Find a—

After a toasted cheese sandwich and a couple of fortifying beers he found himself walking through the red light district. (Found himself? Who are you kidding?) A man in a doorway tried to sell him drugs—'Coke? Crack? You like?'—but Dave waved him away. He was too early for the women. Most of the rooms were shuttered. Two rooms aglow. Crimson for blood? Amber for warning? In the crimson room a heavily made-up blonde sat polishing fearsomely long, lime green fingernails that matched her eye-shadow.

The high stool meant you could see up her short skirt all the way to the place where her thighs joined. Well, almost. And in the second, a brunette: severe, blue eyes, oh no the jutting jaw, the high cheekbones, wearing a few token strips of black leather yet her face reminded him of, almost, of...

I just want to talk. Could I pay you, just to talk? Please? You see, Siggy, I couldn't tell anyone but you but I'm at the end of my...

A bottle of Dutch gin and a street-plan tucked into his Puma bag, he found a cheap hotel on Stadhouders Kade where the noise of the traffic comforted him and the stale smell of the room's last tenant was a kind of reassurance. He laid out the map on the floor and made plans. Mm, the gin was good. Maybe this afternoon he'd stroll by tomorrow's meeting place, then try the Van Gogh Museum or Anne Frank's house. Play the tourist. He lay down on the bed, taking another swig. Eight cigarette burns made a neat circle in the pale blue coverlet. On the wall above the headboard was a cheap reproduction of Van Gogh self-portrait. Here's to you, Vincent.

Art. That's how they'd met: art. Arty people thought you must be stupid if you

234

were a failed publican turned milkman. Whereas, the milkman's friends thought he must be stupid to go to life-drawing classes. That was how he'd seen Siggy naked before he'd even spoken to her. She was modelling to get by: deserted by the husband she'd come to England to marry, stuck with a child and half a set of nursing qualifications in a Council flat. It was thanks to him she'd qualified now: he'd pushed her into it. And what thanks did he get? Eh, Siggy? Nurse Lindstrom?

When he woke it was almost dark outside and he'd been dreaming of being naked himself, surrounded by the scratch of charcoal and the pinpoint-lights of people's eyes, bewildered that Pauline and Jonah had taken up drawing since he last saw them. He was still clutching the gin bottle, half-empty. Some miraculous instinct had made him screw on the top. He propped himself up on his elbow till he'd drunk down the rest of the bottle, and slept again.

The meeting place was at the junction of two canals, at ten a.m. He was there at ten to, strolling casually past over the bridge, pretending to admire the architecture. Nobody seemed to be watching from anywhere. Three strong coffees swished around in his stomach. He

235

squinted, looking up. The sky was brighter today, yet the light somehow flattened the pastel colours of the tall thin houses. What were those hooks and pulleys for, set in the attic walls? And why (yes, think of something, anything but ten o'clock)—why did there seem to be doors at the level above the ground, doors that would open on to nothing? Why hadn't he brought a camera? Commit it to memory, *use your imagination,* five to ten so it's time to turn back. Concentrate on the architecture. No, not the people. There must be thousands of faces in Amsterdam so why did the only ones he passed seem so familiar? That round-faced man pushing his bicycle. That woman in dark glasses and a headscarf. A motor-bike roared past him, over the cobbles. Hadn't it overtaken him going the other way, five minutes before? That same one? He shivered, recalling his nakedness in the dream, touching the sheen of his jacket to make sure he was clothed.

He was at the bridge again, staring nonchalantly into the grey-green waters of Prinsen Gracht. A sightseeing boat ploughed towards him. He turned away, seeing the cameras pointing up. One minute past. A group of young teenagers, in shell-suits and trainers, laughing, ran past, hurling a ball from one to another. Wasn't that the same round-faced man again?

'Hey, meester.'

A dark-faced boy, no more than half his height, barefoot, was tugging at his jacket. 'Not now, son.' But the boy persisted, and Dave fumbled for some loose change.

'Hey, meester Dave,' said the boy. Dave's heart skipped. The boy was smiling, his eyes blinking fast, a tiny clown in rags. Then he turned, and waved for Dave to follow, and began to skip away. Half-running to keep up, Dave scurried through alleys, over bridges, across the Amstel river so they must be heading east, surely? Nothing was familiar now, not the faces, not the houses. There was a tightness in his chest, the boy was teasing him, running ahead almost out of sight, then skipping back, waving, blinking his Chaplin pseudo-smile, running off again.

The chase ended at a houseboat. Grey water splashed against the concrete quay. The boy stood on the deck, his left hand on his chest, and gestured below with his right hand in exaggerated welcome before jumping off and skipping away along the canal bank. Dave took a deep breath. The air smelt dank. The boat was a peeling black, with a fading name in Arabic on the port bow. He stood on the once-polished boards of the deck, now cracked, one or two of them missing, looking uncertainly down the steps. A curtain of beads hid from view whoever was shouting in an unfamiliar language. The voices didn't stop when he jangled through the curtain, peering into the semi-darkness. There were two of them: Moroccans, Algerians? The old one lay in a bunk-bed, wearing a dirty white nightshirt. His face was shrunk to the bones and his hand was skeletal as his finger jabbed the air. Yet his voice was powerful, almost musical, as he shouted at the other, a moustached man of maybe Dave's age dressed in an immaculate blue suit, incongruous here among the dirt and the stench of sickness.

For a full minute the pair of them seemed not even to notice his presence. Then the younger man spat at the older one, and turned. 'Look,' said Dave, shrugging, smiling, 'if I've called at a bad time...'

Now the one in the suit was addressing Dave in a new language. French, yes, French. 'Sorry, je ne comprends pas.'

That brought on another round of Arabic or whatever it was. Dave spread his hands. Finally the man took Dave's bag from his shoulder with a sudden, rough twist—bet you've nicked a few handbags in your time, mate—zipped it open, and, reaching beneath the old man's bunk, stuffed a gift-wrapped parcel in among Dave's guide books and underwear. He zipped up the

238

bag and thrust it into Dave's hands. 'Main-te-nant,' he said slowly, as if speaking to a child, a child younger and more foolish even than the barefoot messenger boy, 'main-te-nant-fuck-off. Vous com-pre-nez?' Then something made the man's gaze flick away to the bed. Dave saw the glint of a knife in the old man's hand. 'Thanks,' said Dave. 'It's really been a pleasure.'

At last he sat in the tiny cabin, soothed by the gentle motion of the sea again, and stared at the package: a half-metre cube, carefully done up in white paper dotted with blue spots, a pink ribbon wound neatly round it, finished off with an elegant bow. Here, Siggy, this is for you: ten grand's worth of gift. Whatever it is. He reached for the bow and—

No. Why look? You know what's in it, don't you? What else would be worth so much that a five-figure fee is just loose change? Wash your face and go for a walk. You haven't eaten for over a day. Whatever you do, don't drink.

Soon he was strolling through the casino, bag slung over his shoulder, double gin in hand. He sat down at a little semi-circular counter; nodded to the croupier. Two cards flicked towards him across the smooth surface. Jack of spades and queen of hearts. You and me, Sig: feeling sentimental, feeling lucky. 'Pay twenty,' said the croupier. Dave doubled his bet. When you owe the taxmen five figures and you're carrying a package worth God knows how many times ten grand, money loses its meaning, right? (Why did he still feel obliged to justify himself? To Pauline, or whoever it was in his head?)

He played for half an hour; came out twenty quid up. He turned to head for the bar. A blonde woman was watching him from the roulette table. No, come on, that's just paranoia, Dave. This one's older. She wasn't on the boat coming over. Quit staring at her. Walk past.

She smiled. Her hand was on his arm. 'You were on the boat coming over.' Neutral accent. Her big hand, warm on his wrist. No ring. 'We must be on the same package.'

I'm not on any package, love, the package is on me. 'Buy you a drink?'

And so it was that at two in the morning they sat side by side in a quiet corner in two red plastic seats, Dave and Irene, holding hands. He'd invited her to his cabin but hadn't minded when she'd said no. Usually he was a listener, that was what drew them to him, like Siggy, like Pauline, at first, that he listened: before they started repeating themselves and he got bored. Tonight, though, he

240

talked—rambled—about himself, about the feeling that a net was closing about him, that this guy he'd loved like a father had turned against him, that familiar people had become strangers while strangers seemed weirdly familiar, how it was like a series of Surrealist paintings, a movie by Salvador Dali, y'know, Dali, do you know what I mean?

Was he even saying these things, or only dreaming them?

He went to sleep there, holding her hand, knowing nothing about her. When he woke the boat was docking at Hull and she was no longer there. A moment's panic: no, the bag was undisturbed, over his arm. He hunted for the woman among the disembarking crowd, but somehow wasn't surprised that he couldn't find her.

He phoned the Leeds number from the station at Hull. A voice that might have been Malik's—it was hostile and condescending enough—gave him an address in Dewsbury to memorise. He phoned Siggy but the answerphone was on and he couldn't think what to say.

He went to the station buffet and ate two bacon and tomato rolls and two cups of foul tea. Someone had left a newspaper at his table and he found himself staring at the headline—"FERGIE'S

BACK!"—unable to fathom its meaning. "TRAVELLER'S FARE" it said on the side of his paper cup. "MEET ME HE..." was scratched into the formica table.

He took the single ticket for his journey from his pocket and scrutinised the letters and numbers, trying to decipher what they might imply.

The Dewsbury address was a shabby, brightly-painted terrace. He'd given the cab-driver a false number but the right street name, and had to walk away from a conversation about why the number didn't exist. The woman who answered the door was hardly more than a child: a very round brown face, encircled by the orange of her chador that extended to the ground. A tiny baby was cradled in her arms. She didn't seem to understand English. 'Ma-lik. Ma-lik,' he was saying. She was shaking her head and trying to close the door but his foot was wedged there. He began to open his bag. She shook her head, her words turning to an odd moaning sound, as she retreated from him into the house. He followed her through the living room into the dark kitchen and showed her the open bag: the gift-wrapped package. She was still shaking her head. The baby began to cry. She stood, her back to the back door, resting her arm on the gas-ring, eyes downcast.

'Please,' he said, 'I don't want to hurt you. Malik sent me. Malik. Malik?'

They were at an impasse. Had he misremembered the address? No, he was sure. He looked round the room. A rug half-covered the floor. There were no chairs: only a low table, with the remains of someone's breakfast on it, and the cooker and fridge and cupboards and hanging saucepans by the door. The baby was wailing now. He sat down on the floor, spread his hands. 'I'll wait for Malik. Okay? Okay?'

She rocked the baby, not looking at Dave.

Get out of here, man. Call Pauline and say you're sorry. Call Siggy and tell her you love her and you want to go to Sweden and make a new start and throw the package into the nearest litter bin. Right?'

Ten minutes later they were still fixed in their tableau—him on the floor, cross-legged, stiffening; her wedged against the cooker, the baby sleeping again now in her arms—when the front door went and a young Asian man came in. His eyes took in the scene for a moment; the young woman babbled at him; he grabbed a saucepan from the wall and approached Dave. Dave raised his hands in surrender, 'Hey, hey, Malik sent me.'

'Malik? Who Malik?'

'He said to bring this package here,' careful not to move, simply nodding towards the pink ribbon round the blue-spotted wrapping paper.

The man curled his fingers inside the bag; pulled it towards him, out of Dave's reach. 'And what is in this—this package?'

Dave felt incredibly calm. 'Don't ask me, mate. I'm only the delivery man. Mind if I go now?'

'Stay!'

'Woof,' said Dave.

But he stayed, even though the man had put down the saucepan so that he could rip the package apart with both his thin hands. It was full of plastic bags of white powder. The man held one out to his wife, to Dave; let out a howl. 'I tell Salim, no more!' His eyes were darting to left and right: 'Salim sends you?'

'Malik,' said Dave, trying to edge towards the door. But the man picked up the saucepan, jabbering something to his wife, then turned to threaten Dave again: 'Is trap. I tell Salim, no more. But Salim says this thing must continue or...or...'

Suddenly there was a pounding at the back door. The young woman leapt away

244

from it, screaming, clutching the baby. There was a more distant banging from the front. 'Open up! Police!'

The regular guy can't make this trip. Suddenly Dave understood what it was he was delivering: himself. Himself and—

'You bastard!' screeched the Asian man, face screwed up in terror and anger, hitting him on the crown of the head with the saucepan. Dave rolled over, not defending himself, sniggering at the echo of the saucepan's impact on his head, feeling an overwhelming sense of release. He was sure he was smiling. This was what a ten grand write-off was worth: two sacrificial victims, two pathetic fall guys set up with a token consignment and, presumably, an anonymous 999 call, so that Jonah and a man whose name probably wasn't Malik could keep their sordid little business out of reach of the long arm of the law.

Siggy, I've been a bloody idiot but if you'll wait for me, when I get out, no I mean it this time, why don't we go to Sweden and...

'Let them in,' he said. 'There'll be a blonde woman with them. And a round-faced guy on a bike.' The woman's screams and the pounding drowned out his words but it seemed important to keep trying to explain: 'There's nothing we can do, you see. My dada sent them.'

11

A Quiet Evening at Fountains
by
STEPHEN MURRAY

Fountains Abbey: glorious relic of ecclesiastical splendour; immemorial resort for Yorkshire trippers; World Heritage Site. Imposing ruins, ornamental water gardens, woodland walks, rustic valleys.

Bank Holiday Monday: obligatory leisure; day of pleasure. Uncovered torsos, ice creams, jammed roads, ordeal by proximity, family test.

Bank Holiday Monday at Fountains Abbey.

To be rostered for Bank Holiday Monday, Liz reflected as she let herself be carried along by the flow, would be regarded by many of her fellow voluntary wardens as drawing the short straw.

True, the rest of the year the wardens spent more time helping the disorientated than restraining the antisocial (though the demon diggers-up of wild flower plants sometimes cut up unrepentantly rough).

True, Bank Holiday visitors seemed to regard Fountains Abbey as a Theme Park—ruins thoughtfully erected for climbing; sward mown for family football; the crescent ponds dug expressly for shrimping nets. She had even glimpsed a little horror taking pot-shots at the ducks with a catapult—egged on by his fond father—but they had moved on before her middle-aged limbs could catch up with them. And true, to be so often having to rein in thoughtlessness could be dispiriting.

But there was something endearing about the Bank Holiday crowds nonetheless. Liz diverged to the little arbour which gave a vista over the water gardens towards the Octagon Tower on the hilltop, and let her gaze follow the crowds idling along the canal. So many people in search of so simple a thing—a few hours' peace—and with the odds so heavily stacked against them. Long journeys, fractious children, carping in-laws. That family passing below her right now, for example: hot, harassed mother; complaining children dragging their feet; father threatening clips round the ear. Their various moans and snaps ascended only too clearly to her ears. They had come here for something that was hard enough to find, in all conscience, in today's world. Why grudge them a little clumsiness in their search?

Returning from her reverie, Liz reinstated herself in the stream of ambling people and soon came to the rustic bridge—automatically checking dogs on lead, no-one paddling in the lake away to the right, children not getting too friendly with unpredictable swans—and let herself be carried round in the direction of Studley Royal. As she did so, she saw an upright, unmistakable figure bustling towards her.

Joe Watson. Well, he was endearing too, in his way, regarding Fountains so terribly proprietorially. He took every negligent misbehaviour as a personal affront, interpreted every thoughtlessness as deliberate vandalism. Yet in private life he was the soul of generosity and bonhomie. Not to visitors, though! They had best watch their step when Joe was wardening!

Liz's heart sank a little as she observed Joe's pursed lips of outrage and purposeful gait. His expression sharpened as he spotted her, and he thrust across the idling stream to accost her. Liz found herself searching her memory for personal shortcomings.

'Ah, there you are!'

'Here I am, Joe,' she agreed meekly.

'Come with me!'

And he turned and marched off the

way he had come, and Liz with a little hop and a skip caught up with him and trotted at his side, wondering what she was about to have to sort out. As they passed the Temple of Piety she crossed her fingers surreptitiously. Joe could be so confrontational sometimes, in his zeal for Fountains.

Joe turned up the path towards the Octagon Tower, only to stop abruptly a hundred yards along, bouncing on his toes. Across the ornamental lakes on the further slopes the Banqueting House peeped among the rich foliage. Further along, the painted arbour where Liz had been only twenty minutes before glinted in the sun.

'There!' Joe announced.

Liz followed the direction of his gaze as best she could.

'I'm sorry, Joe,' she said. 'My eyes aren't what they were.'

'*There!* Just down there.'

Liz looked where Joe pointed, and saw the scandal. Someone had sought out on the wooded bank just beneath them a sheltered nook to sunbathe in. It was an area not exactly forbidden to visitors—there were no barriers—but where the paths were laid out to discourage excursions off the marked way. It was always a shame to have to evict people from the few areas denied them. Necessary, of course, because others would swiftly follow on the "they're doing it so why can't I?" principle—but Liz always regretted the necessity.

A quiet spot; a young couple, probably, though she couldn't see very clearly. Liz's soft heart found ready sympathy for them. But she knew better than to waste effort trying to get Joe to share her view. They were, he was quite right, where they should not be.

'But Joe, it's not like you to be backward.' She risked teasing him a little.

Joe tutted, which meant she was being more than usually obtuse; but he seemed unaccustomedly embarrassed too. Liz screwed up her eyes and looked again through the dappled light and shade of the high summer foliage. She could only see one figure, now she looked carefully. So unlike Joe to be afraid of...

'Oh, Joe!' She laughed delightedly. 'Oh dear, poor you!'

'You may laugh,' Joe bridled. 'This place gets more like Brighton beach every weekend. If she wants to lie around like that, what does she want to come here for? No respect, these Bank Holiday people. No respect at all!'

'Alright, Joe. I'll go and ask her to put something on. And tell her she must find another spot.'

'Right. Right.'

But some malicious imp in Liz made her say, 'You'd better come with me though, Joe. Otherwise I might not be firm enough!'

'Well, I...'

'Alright. You stay here. You can stop anyone else following me when they see me walking where I shouldn't.'

And Liz stepped off the path and began to pick her careful way down the steep slope, leaving Joe placed squarely as a sentinel and giggling to herself at his predicament. He was a bit of a dear, Joe, for all his prickliness. Too gentlemanly to be able to approach a topless sunbather. What *would* the ghosts of the monks of Fountains Abbey be saying, as they looked down on the little drama? She fancied they might be chuckling, just a little.

She composed her features as she drew near. The girl seemed to be asleep: unaware of her approach, at any rate. Liz didn't want to startle her. She could see her more clearly now. A pretty girl, slim, with her dark hair spread fanlike round her upturned head, looking so vulnerable, asleep like that.

At least: she *was* asleep, wasn't she? Or shamming because she'd spotted the approach of authority? There was something a little theatrical about her abandoned limbs. And—her eyes were open, after all! And her hair couldn't be dark, because it glistened like gold on her forehead.

And if that wasn't hair spread beneath her head, then...

'Joe! *Joe!*'

Liz shouted as she had not shouted since she used to coach lacrosse, before her retirement, before Fountains; and her blood quickened and her brain snapped into full gear as it had used to so easily in those days of schoolmistressly authority. She barely waited to see Joe step over the distant rope before she was scrambling the last few yards to the recumbent figure, already ordering the sequence of her actions.

So much blood! But was she alive? Liz laid the back of her hand against the girl's breast—better not touch the face—and felt it warm; but the sun was beating down on this sheltered nook and that might mean nothing. She moved her head, feeling now for the heartbeat, even as she registered that the blood was sticky and the eyes dull.

Behind her she heard Joe crashing through the undergrowth and the next moment he—bless him, when it came to the crunch all his fussiness slipped away, and with his keener sight he had already seen what she had only seen when close to—was kneeling by her side, feeling in his turn for a pulse, letting his eyes travel—as Liz had not quite—to the wound and over it.

'She's dead,' Liz said calmly.

'Yes,' replied Joe.

'And so pretty,' Liz said inconsequentially. 'Who could do such a thing?'

'And here!' Joe could not help protesting. 'Who could do such a thing here?'

Looking back the way they had come, Liz saw that a family was already pausing on the pathway and preparing to follow them down the hillside—so much more fun than sticking to the path. She touched Joe's arm and he looked up.

'Stay here,' he ordered tersely. 'Don't move and don't let *anyone* come close. I'll get help.' He clambered to his feet. 'Hey, *you!* Get back on that path *at once!*' And he scrambled swiftly up the hillside to fend them off.

Liz watched him for a moment, saw him meet the family, saw them all turn back down the path; saw Joe gesticulating; saw a young man detach himself from the group and run off purposefully. You could rely on Joe. He would do his part. She must do hers.

And she turned back, with no repulsion or horror now, and contemplated with sorrow the young woman who lay dead on the brightly coloured rug in the Bank Holiday sun.

'A nightmare!'

'Never mind,' replied Detective Chief Superintended Whittle. 'Tell me what you've done so far.'

They were the only two figures strolling on the path by the Temple of Piety. A hundred yards away vehicles clustered at the foot of the track which led to the Octagon Tower. An ambulance and the pathologist's car had backed up the track so as to be only a short distance from the body.

'We put men on the gates, of course,' Detective Chief Inspector Langley said gloomily. 'Allowed people out—as far as their cars—closed the exit to the car-parks—turned away new arrivals. There are traffic jams,' he added bitterly, 'from here to Harrogate.'

'Never mind.'

'This place is like a sieve. For someone on foot, there are a dozen ways out. And whoever it was was probably long gone before ever that old trout found the body.'

'And who is the old trout?'

'A Miss Elizabeth Atkinson. Retired schoolteacher. You know the sort.'

'The sort?'

'Well...' Langley drew the word out, expressively and with an edge of derision. 'Still, she seems to have kept her head. And the other chap's a bloke called Joseph Watson. Tore a strip off the doctor good and proper for driving his Volvo over the grass. By the way, seems you're not supposed to even bloody *walk* on the bit where the body is.'

'No?'

'No.'

The superintendent climbed up to where the pathologist sat in the offending Volvo, doors agape to the beneficent sun, dictating his preliminary report.

'Afternoon, Bob.'

'Afternoon, Terry.'

'Well?'

'Well, fractured skull, unconscious at once, death within a few minutes.'

'Rather a lot of blood?'

The pathologist nodded philosophically. 'It happens.'

'Where was she hit?'

'Here.' The doctor fingered his own skull, on the very top where the hair had cleared a tonsure. 'Sharp stone, about half a pound in weight, delivered with a good deal of force.'

The policeman raised his eyebrows expressively. The pathologist grinned. 'No magic. It was lying by the body.'

'Shenanigans?' This was the superintendent's invariable way of enquiring about sexual interference.

'Nope. Not a mark on her other than the wound which killed her.'

'Time, then?'

The other man narrowed his eyes to the sun like a farmer gauging lunchtime. 'Hour and a half before I saw her? Not less, could be more in this heat.'

Fifty yards away the undertakers were fetching a plastic body-bag out of their van. The two men walked over to watch the process of loading, in case anything of interest should be revealed as the body was moved. Nothing was. Both men looked instinctively up at the Octagon Tower, beetling above them melodramatically.

'You know what I'm thinking?'

'Me too.'

'We'll match the stone, if that's the case,' Whittle said.

'She's sitting up, kids up there, they can't resist the target, loose piece of stone lying about, Bob's your uncle.' The pathologist sketched the scene out quickly and graphically.

Whittle looked down and saw Miss Atkinson sitting on the grass by the lake, her hands clasped round her bent knees. Her pale face was raised, watching them. She looked younger than he expected, and he felt a spurt of bitter anger at Langley referring to her as an old trout. He made his way down the path and went across and sat down beside her. He was very tall, and seemed to have to fold himself up like a pair of dividers before he could reach ground level.

'A bad business.'

She merely nodded, her eyes on the undertakers loading the anonymous bundle into their van. As the doors shut she said, 'Such a pretty girl.'

'You found her, I believe.'

'Yes; at least, I found her *dead,* if that's what you mean. Joe Watson—have you spoken to Joe?—saw her first, and asked if I would come across and have a word with her. Poor Joe!' She smiled wanly. 'If she could only have known it, she had found the only way to ensure herself against his wrath. She shouldn't have been there, of course. Not where she was.'

'You hadn't spotted her earlier? I'm wondering whether there was any one with her.'

'There are nobody else's things with hers, are there?'

'You noticed that?'

'The ones who seek out the quiet spots, it's usually couples. Who can blame them? When you're young...'

'But she was alone.'

'Just lying there. When Joe pointed her out she looked so peaceful I really hated myself for being about to disturb her. I'm rather short-sighted, you see,' she said apologetically. 'It wasn't until I was quite close that I saw that...that it wasn't like that at all.'

'And you hadn't seen her before, on your rounds?'

She shook her head regretfully. 'I was down at the Abbey all the time. I just strolled up here for a break and met Joe, and he asked me if I could help.'

'Well, thank you. I'll send an officer over to take a statement from you. I'm sorry you've had to wait around. Sorry you've had to experience all this.' The undertakers' van was moving warily down the track. It lurched round the corner onto the main path and drove off towards the distant gates.

'You'll never find out who did it, will you?'

'Oh, come now! Yes, of course we will. That's an absurd thing to say at this stage,' Whittle protested with a confidence he was a long way from feeling.

'No. How can you? So many people... She was such a pretty girl; and such a beautiful day.'

After the superintendent had left her, Liz sat on, staring out over the water garden towards the distant slopes where the sun winked on the cars in the car park, full of hot, angry, bewildered trippers penned there until they could be questioned and released. Such a beautiful day!

After a while a young policewoman came over and took her statement with slightly patronising consideration. Liz, who had felt quite young in the superintendent's company, suddenly felt old again and saw herself through this girl's eyes: a retired schoolmistress, doing voluntary work to fill her days harmlessly.

'Thank you,' the policewoman smiled. 'I've got your address. You're free to go now if you like.'

'How will I get out?' Liz asked.

'I'll radio through to the car park, and they'll see you right.'

'I'll have to call in to the office first.'

'Whatever.'

It was very peaceful away from the cluster of cars and the purposeful to-ing and fro-ing of policemen. The grounds were deserted. Liz saw Fountains as she had not seen it even on the most deserted of winters' days. She walked slowly round by the lake until the Abbey came into sight. Rearing majestically even in ruins, where it had stood through the centuries by the waters of the Skell, it seemed to represent verities capable of making sense even of the ultimate chaos of sudden death. Liz sat on one of the wayside seats and gazed at those strangely comforting grey ruins. Almost, an onlooker might have thought, as if listening to them.

She rose and turned reluctantly back. Where the ways divided she forked left, away from the Temple of Piety, crossing the rustic bridge and taking the path to the arbour where she had stood only a few short hours ago. The sun was still as high in the sky; the shadows had only shifted a little round the compass.

Now the arbour was deserted, and she sat down on its wooden seat. The banks of the canal were bare now: no strolling couples, no darting children, no brightly coloured clothes and reddening limbs. Moorhens nosed into the bank and three swans sailed placid and uncaring upon their own reflections. Only, across the valley, those official cars, those indistinct bustling figures beneath the Octagon Tower.

After a few moments Joe came and sat beside her.

'What have you done with the catapult?' she asked.

He paused just too long before repeating: 'Catapult?'

'Oh, Joe!' It was said sorrowfully. After a while she said: 'I suppose you never had one; as a boy, I mean.'

'As it happens, no. Though I don't for the life of me know what you're getting at.'

'Oh, Joe,' she said again sadly.

She looked back through time to what seemed improbable days: herself as a tomboy, roaming through the overgrown garden of a deserted mansion in Headingley, an honorary member of the local gang of toughs, tolerated for her access to knicker elastic. She couldn't see Joe, dear formal overzealous Joe in any gang, in scruffy shorts, with scabbed knees. But she could see so clearly how it had been this afternoon. His shocked affront when he spotted the girl. Liz almost persuaded herself she had heard his initial shout of reprimand. She could see him set off towards the girl to reinforce the message, realise her state of undress and stop abruptly.

'You shouted and shouted, of course.'

Joe said: 'It didn't make any difference. She just lay there, ignoring me. Where she shouldn't be.'

'And you wondered how to make her take notice, and you remembered you had just the thing: you had the catapult. I saw him, the young idiot, shooting at the ducks with it, and I was too slow, too far off, to catch up with him. But later they passed me, that family, and the child was whining because his catapult had been taken away. By you, Joe.'

'Go on.'

'That's why I say you never had one as a boy. If you had, you'd have known. Knicker elastic makes a lethal weapon, Joe.'

'It wasn't knicker elastic. It looked—very professional.'

'And you thought it was the ideal way to make her take notice. Because you dare not go up to her, as you would to anyone else, to tick her off.'

'How could I?'

Liz turned and looked at him, reliable, zealous Joe, in his cavalry twill slacks and his tie and his white linen jacket, with his neat greying hair, who had fought fearlessly in war and met his match in an innocent girl sunbathing on a hot Bank Holiday, and said again, 'Poor Joe.'

'You were here. You saw what happened?'

'I was here.'

She did not say that her sight was not up to picking out brief flashes of action across the other side of the valley. Instead she opened her hand to disclose the tiny deaf aid she had taken from where it had lain on the girl's discarded shirt. Without looking at it, she placed it carefully on the seat between them.

After a while, he said, 'What are you going to do?'

And Liz could not answer. She had been asking herself that question ever since the superintendent had looked up at the Octagon Tower and she had realised he was speculating about kids and stones. She hadn't *seen* anything—how could she, with her poor sight? Joe had made no confession. The catapult was probably at the bottom of one of the lakes. She turned to Joe to say that she didn't know: but he had gone; and so had the deaf aid.

For a while she wondered whether she had done the right thing; whether she had interpreted aright what the Abbey had seemed to be saying to her. She strained her eyes towards the knot of uniformed and plain-clothed figures still bustling between the cluster of vehicles and the little piece of woodland on the further slope; but they were too far off for her to distinguish. She *thought* she saw a stiff-backed figure go up to a very tall one, but perhaps it was just wishful thinking. After a while some people got into one of the cars and it drove away.

A long time after, the other figures began to drift back to the vehicles, and they started to leave.

Liz sat on in the arbour until they had all departed. The vague noises from the

263

direction of the car park ceased. The sun was lower in the sky now but it was still hot, and the air was very still. The water in the canal and in the ornamental lakes glinted dully like pewter. The water fowl widened the circle of their grazing. Pheasant waddled down on to the mown lawns and began pecking about. Liz reflected ruefully that she would never see a quieter Bank Holiday evening at Fountains.

Then all at once a flock of geese appeared low in the sky from the direction of the Abby, gliding in grey and silent on the still air. As they neared the water they checked their flight in an explosive clapping of their wings, shattering the oppressive silence.

But Liz heard it as the sound of monks applauding.

Author's Note

I have a special interest in this case. It began in April, 1949, when, as a brand new police recruit, I was taken to see the "Black Museum" at Stanley Grange, Hoghton, near Preston, where the Lancashire Constabulary Training School had its base.

Among the blood-stained razors, garottes, drugs and instruments of perversion on display I noticed a pair of shoes of truly grand proportions: they were at least twice as big as my own size tens. From a printed card alongside, I learned that they had been the property of Reuben Mort, a retired blacksmith and ironmonger, who had been murdered at Little Lever, near Bolton, thirty years before. No murder file was supplied—not even a potted account—and yet it was 'Owd Reuben's' story above all the others that took my curiosity. "Mort" meant death, and I could see the tiny irony in that, but I'm sure it was the shoes that impressed me most. During the remainder of my training, whenever I passed the museum building I would look up at the windows and speculate about the poor old man who must have been a giant to have needed such footwear.

Years later, in 1988, I had the chance to find out more about the Reuben Mort case. I was researching for a book of factual Lancashire murders and had been given permission to search through the records at Police Headquarters. There was an index containing a reference to the murder, but the file of evidence was missing. All I could discover from the index was that a man called Joseph Thomas McHugh had confessed to the murder.

So I shelved "Mort" in favour of more interesting cases and it was only after I had completed *Murder in Lancashire* and sent the typescript to my publishers that once again I began to wonder if the "Blacksmith" story might be worth pursuing. I took the obvious course of writing to the press. The editor of Bolton Evening News, typical of his kind, sent me a friendly and helpful letter including photostats of two items bearing on the case. There were an editor's reply to "Wondering" of Little Lever, dated May, 1960, and an article by James Ryan, entitled "Murder That Shocked a Village" which had been published in the Farnworth Journal, part of the Bolton Evening News group. Mr Ryan's article had been timed to appear on 20th January, 1970—the fiftieth anniversary of Reuben Mort's death.

I was delighted to have them because they told me a great deal about the murder, yet neither of the accounts completely answered my needs. The first declared: "Neither the murderer nor the murder weapon were ever traced," whilst the second described the murder of Mort as "Still unsolved after half a century."

How could this be, when I knew the name of the man who had confessed? Much intrigued, I began a serious search for further information, and from what I learned from several sources I am able to tell the story that follows.

12

The Village Blacksmith Murder
by
ALAN SEWART

At the time of his death, Reuben Mort was 78 years old and retired from business. His heyday had been years earlier, when horse-owners from miles around had brought their animals to be shod at his smithy, and most of the residents of the village owed their gates, railings, fire-irons and metal utensils to Mort's skill at the anvil. As a flourishing tradesman he was able to buy property in the village, including his own house and shop at 3 Market Street, Little Lever. For many years he was a sidesman at St Matthew's Church and his face was also well-known at the Little Lever Conservative Club. For six years, until reaching the age of 70, he served on the Little Lever Urban District Council. After that, feeling no doubt he had done enough, he settled down in his home and rarely left it again for the rest of his life.

Not surprisingly, the old man soon acquired the reputation of being a recluse: arm-in-arm with that went a more material reputation, that of being a rich man who kept a large sum of money in his house. It seems certain that the man who entered the house on 19th/20th January, 1920 was seeking Reuben's money. Indeed, he actually said so, according to Reuben's version.

The first intimation of the attack came about four o'clock in the morning, when John Thomas Lomax, who ran a tripe shop next door at 1, Market Street, heard Mort banging on their communal wall. Asked about it later, Lomax said he "didn't feel too concerned at first," but the way he responded seems to belie that assertion.

He roused his wife, they both got up and dressed, and going out of the house they went *not* next door but to Fletcher Street, some distance away, where lived Mort's one-time housekeeper, Mrs Davies. Only then did they go round the back of Mort's house, with Mrs Davies leading the way. They knew the glass was missing from a small back window (it had been broken in recent gales and not repaired) and arriving at the window they shouted through it.

'Is that you?' Mort shouted. 'I'm fain you've come.' and he dragged himself to the back door, opened it and let his neighbours in. As they entered he collapsed on the floor. They could see he was badly wounded about the head. The floor of the back room was heavily splashed with blood.

Though weak from loss of blood, Mort was able to give a coherent account of what had happened. Following a habit, he had come downstairs from his bedroom in the early hours of the morning to make himself a cup of tea. Whilst he was boiling the kettle a man had suddenly appeared in the room and demanded the keys to his safe. Mort had told the man he "didn't have the keys on him," whereupon the man had produced a heavy weapon of some sort and begun striking him about the head and shoulders. As the attack was continuing he had lost consciousness and could remember no more. Some time later, when he came to his senses, his assailant had gone. He had then hammered on the wall to waken John Lomax.

He described the intruder as "a big man" but did not name him, so (by implication at least) he was a stranger. Since there was no sign of forcible entry to the house it was concluded that the attacker had climbed in through the broken window and, as the window was "quite small", one theory was that the man could not have been "big" as Mort suggested. However, as any burglar might testify, it is quite remarkable how small a space a "big" man can squeeze through. Mort himself was a big man, as evidenced by the shoes later to be displayed in the museum, and in spite of his age he would surely have been able to offer more resistance had his attacker been small.

As Mort told his story he was growing weaker. The local G.P, Doctor Nuttall, had already been sent for and shortly after his arrival he ordered that the injured man should be taken at once to Bolton Infirmary. Efforts were made to save him but his injuries were too great. He lingered for more than twelve hours and died about 6.30 p.m on the same day. Following a post mortem examination, cause of death was given as "internal haemorrhage due to serious head injuries."

Police officers called to investigate found there was some ransacking inside the house but apart from the murder weapon nothing was known to be missing. In view of Mort's reported comment that the attacker had demanded the safe keys, a search was made for them and they were soon found—lying on a ledge in the stair-well in plain sight of anyone who happened to look. The attacker had not seen them, or surely he would have opened the safe and stolen the contents, about two thousand pounds in money which the police found still inside.

So the attacker had got away with nothing—and perhaps he had left something of himself behind. Experts from the fingerprint department dusted the furniture and other suitable surfaces, raising a broad assortment of latent prints. These were developed and photographed for comparison. Beginning with Reuben Mort himself, all people with known and legitimate access to the house were asked to supply fingerprints for comparison and elimination and when this line of enquiry was exhausted, the few outstanding fingerprints were presumed likely to be those of the attacker. They were placed in the "scenes of crime" file at Police Headquarters.

Some days later—on 25th or 26th January—Police Constable Snidell of the West Riding Constabulary took a set of six photographs of Mort's house on behalf of the Lancashire Constabulary.

Police confidence ran high that an arrest would soon be made, but as the period of investigation lengthened and no more clues were found it began to be feared that Reuben Mort's killer would not be brought to justice. Rumours were rife in the village. One popular feeling publicly voiced was that he must be a local man because he had known that Mort kept money in a safe, but this was offset somewhat by the fact that Mort did not recognise his attacker.

But the rumours persisted. Relatives had committed the crime to speed their inheritance. Men had suddenly left the village, never to return. At least one anonymous letter naming the killer was received by the police, but they were easily able to establish that the named man could not have been involved. The announcement of a reward of £100 for information leading to the arrest of the killer brought a fresh flood of helpful suggestions but not one was found to have foundation.

Reuben Mort was buried on Friday, 23rd January, in St Matthew's Churchyard and the funeral is said to have been marked by a curious event. Some credence had been given to a local prophecy that the guilty man would be indicated by some supernatural sign—a sort of heavenly adjudication—and the prophet must have felt vindicated by what happened. The cortège stood in line outside 88 High Street, Little Lever, the home of Mort's nephew, J W Stringfellow and family—and when the time came to move off, the horses drawing the first coach refused to budge. A deal of cajolery left them unmoved and in great frustration the passengers had to climb out and follow the hearse on foot.

When the inquest was held on 21st January, 1920, it was made clear that the rumours had not gone unnoticed. The Coroner, Mr J Fearnley, opened by pouring scorn on "...all sorts of silly, idiotic rumours that such and such person has done it...even that his relatives have done it." After calling witnesses he recorded a verdict of "Murder—by some person or persons unknown."

Police enquiries continued for some time afterwards. Indeed, in theory they never ended, since some aspects of an undetected murder (outstanding fingerprints, subsequent crimes with similarities, casual snippets of new information from almost any source) are always processed and tested in the search for vital links. But after the known pointers had been followed as far as they led and all likely suspects had been eliminated, the police scaled the investigation down, leaving the file "open, but inactive."

Writing in 1970, James Ryan says firmly:

...now the murder that shook Little Lever to its foundation is almost forgotten, except by the older generation. Occasionally the crime is the subject of conversations locally and older people will say: 'Oh yes, old Reuben Mort!' But for the most part, younger people comment: 'Reuben Mort? Who was he?'

And he concludes by saying:

The murderer may still be alive, carrying his grim secret on his conscience: a secret that will go with him to the grave.

Perhaps so—and perhaps not so!

Almost six years after the murder happened, the Reuben Mort case had resurfaced in a most dramatic way. It cannot be claimed that any investigative police action brought this about. The initiative came from Joseph Thomas McHugh. McHugh was then 27 years of age and a native of Farnworth, near Bolton: a township only a mile or so from Little Lever. His settled home was with his wife, Lily, at 13A Princess Street, Farnworth, but he was a wanderer by nature. Standing five-feet-ten-inches tall and with stocky build he was "big" enough to answer Mort's description of his attacker, but it was not the Mort case that McHugh initially brought to light.

When, on 1st November 1925, he walked into the police station at Mullingar, Westmeath, Ireland, McHugh wanted to give himself up for an entirely different case of murder. He told the police that a month earlier, on 2nd October, 1925, he had met a young woman at Pendleton, Salford and had strangled her, afterwards throwing her body into the canal at Pendleton. He said he could not name the woman or describe the place where he committed the crime.

Four days later on 5th November (extradition from Ireland to the United Kingdom took time, even in those days) McHugh was handed over to detectives from Salford City Police and after appearing briefly at the City Magistrates' Court he was remanded to Manchester Prison until 12th November. While he languished, the police were busy trying to verify his claims. A long and tedious search of canals in the Salford area failed to produce a body and of the people listed as missing persons, both locally and at Scotland Yard, none seemed to compare with McHugh's description. McHugh was taken on a tour of the district and seemed to be trying to remember details of his walk with the unknown woman, but the sum of his efforts was inconclusive.

Nevertheless, on 12th November, 1925, he was brought before the stipendiary magistrate at Salford on a charge of murder, and whilst sitting in court he made another revelation. Beckoning to Police Sergeant Arthur Wood, he said: 'Here. Hand this up to yon fellow.'

"Yon fellow" was the magistrate and "this" was a self-written statement that read as follows:

Sir—First of all let me say that I plead guilty and that all I wish and expect is that you will do your duty in the quickest possible manner. I am 27 years of age and last worked as a platelayer for the L.M.S.R [London, Midland and Scottish Railway]. I joined the army when I was 15 years of age and served on active service in France being wounded and gassed. Since the end of the war things have not gone too well with me what with being bad with my head and my stomach and having bad luck with her who calls herself my wife it seems as

276

though everything has been against me. But to come back to the matter in hand I want you all to understand that I don't ask for pity of any kind. I did at first think of asking for aid to defend me but I am now sure that it will be best otherwise therefore the only thing I ask nay even implore of you is that you will do away with all minor details and hurry this job on to the best of your ability. Let justice be done. I killed the girl by choking her and then throwing her into the canal, therefore see to it that you avenge the crime by doing your duty which will be of course to pass the death sentence and please let it be clearly understood that such things as appeals etc please keep for those who wish to live a few years longer, for life for me is nothing only a nightmare and the sooner it is over the better it will be for myself and all who are anyway concerned with me.

At this stage McHugh seems to have come to the end of his subject but, undaunted, he presses straight on with another. This time it concerns the main story:

I think also that it will be as well to help the police clear up another matter which has been beyond them. It was I who killed old Reuben Mort of Little

Lever and now having confessed I leave it to you to clear it up. The police they think they are awfully clever but they can make mistakes just the same and I can only say I am sorry that I have not got time to finish off two or three more whom I have got in mind. I really wish now that I had done it before I came here because the world would be more cleaner without them. So once again asking you to get this over as soon as possible.

(Signed) Joseph Thomas McHugh

The tone of this statement is curious. Was this a man who, driven by an urge to be punished, had trumped up a fictitious crime in order to bring that end about? And had he perhaps, because things were not going as well as he had hoped, decided to invoke a real murder and claim responsibility for it, adding the lines about other murders, planned but not yet committed, in order to give himself the aura of an early serial killer?

That is one possibility. At the other extreme is the proposition that McHugh had indeed murdered twice. The police failure to locate a missing woman is not so very surprising. Some people go missing deliberately and hide their tracks because they don't wish to be found: and when many miles of weedy canals are involved, bodies can and do defy discovery.

But convictions are secured on evidence and it seems there was no real evidence to convict McHugh of murder in Salford. He was remanded back to prison until 19th November and ordered to be kept under observation by the prison Medical Officer. On 19th November the doctor testified that he could find nothing wrong with McHugh and that he was of sound mind. Nevertheless, it was decided that no evidence should be offered against him in the Salford case.

What was to be done about the second part of his confession?

The Chief Constable of Lancashire, Mr (later Sir) Philip Lane, took personal responsibility for the case. In a letter to the superintendent at Bolton Division he gave these instructions:

1 Send Shuttleworth [Det Insp] to get McHugh.

2 Charge him on his own confession with the murder of Mort.

3 *Before that:* caution McHugh in accordance with the instructions of His Majesty's Judges of the King's Bench

Division, beginning: "I am informed that you have confessed..."

4 Have the prisoner remanded in custody for sufficient time for him to be fingerprinted and forward his fingerprints to the West Riding Constabulary, along with the six envelopes [photographs of the scene, held on file] with a request that they be compared with those prints taken from furniture, etc at Reuben Mort's house. If none of them compare with McHugh's fingerprints, then when he is brought up again at court you should be prepared to give the evidence of the person from Salford to whom he handed this confession and put in as evidence the original confession, signed by himself: and if you have not been able to obtain any further evidence, inform the court accordingly and *leave it to them* to decide what should be done with him.

(Signed) P Lane.
Chief Constable.

Detective Inspector George Shuttleworth followed these instructions almost to the letter, taking McHugh into custody from the Salford City Police at 12 noon on Friday, 20th November, 1925. Soon afterwards, at Bolton County Police Office

(Castle Street) he formally cautioned and charged him with the murder of Reuben Mort. In reply, McHugh said: 'I have nothing to say at present.' He was brought before the Magistrates' Court and remanded in police custody for three days.

Before long, McHugh decided that he had something to say. At 2.30 p.m on Sunday, 22nd November, Inspector Shuttleworth was informed that the prisoner had a message for him. Going to McHugh's cell he spoke through the door-flap, saying, 'Do you want to see me?'

'Yes,' McHugh told him. 'I want to write a statement.'

The inspector went through the recognised procedure of cautioning McHugh, then handed him a pen and a sheet of paper. McHugh wrote unaided and afterwards handed in the following:

I, Joseph Thomas McHugh do state that I about 2 a.m on the morning of the 20th January, 1920, did murder one Reuben Mort of Market Street, Little Lever. I arrived at the house between the hour of 11.45 p.m and 12.0 m.n going by the way from Glynne Street, Farnworth where I left my wife at her house. (I was then keeping company) I left her about 10.30 p.m on the 19th

281

after having bother with her, went down Egerton Street, Hall Lane, where I stood talking awhile with a friend of mine then went right along past Potters Works to the house which stands alone on the right side of the road. I knocked twice and received no answer. I tried the house window which was loose and entered by it. We both sat talking and after a while we both got falling out when I struck him. I then left him lying on the floor in front of the fireplace and came out again by the window and came home the other way by the Nob Inn, up Wilsons Brow past St Johns Church, Albert Street, Lord Street, and arrived home [12 Ann Street, Kearsley, where he then lived] about 3.0 a.m. I was let in the house by my mother after knocking them up and I then burned my shirt and waistcoat explaining to my mother's questions that I had been fighting. I did not go out of the house again until the following Saturday and on the next day Sunday I had trouble again with my wife because I would not go with her to Little Lever to look at the house [Mort's house]. She went with a friend and I went home again about 3.0 p.m in the afternoon and I did not see her again until the Wednesday.

This is all I wish to say at present it is a true statement and I make it of my own free will having first been warned and cautioned by Inspector Shuttleworth before I made it that I had no need to make it and that it may be used in evidence and that I clearly understand what I am doing.

(Signed) Joseph Thomas McHugh.

This statement by McHugh led to a number of new enquires. Inspector Shuttleworth and his team went to 13A Princess Street, Farnworth, where they interviewed the prisoner's wife, Lily McHugh. She agreed that at the time of the murder she and McHugh had been "keeping company" but that superficial detail was all she would confirm. They had married on 4th September, 1920, some months after the murder. McHugh had been 23 at the time and living with his mother at 12 Ann Street, Kearsley. She had no recollection of having a row with McHugh on the evening before the murder—or having been parted from him because he would not go with her to see the murder house at Little Lever.

Visiting 12 Anne Street, Kearsley, detectives spoke to Mrs Fanny Shrewsbury, McHugh's mother. She roundly denied everything McHugh had written in his statement. She had not been aroused in the small hours, following the murder, to admit her son. He had not burned any of his clothes to her knowledge. It followed that she had not questioned him about bloodstains and he had not said anything to her about being involved in a fight.

And there were discrepancies in McHugh's words too.

"...the house...which stand alone on the right side of the road..." does not accurately describe Reuben Mort's house as it was then. No 3 Market Street, Little Lever, faced Coronation Square and was only semi-detached. The Lomax tripe shop, No 1 Market Street, formed the other half of the pair. On the other side of No 3, there was an entry about five feet wide, with other houses beyond the entry. Of course, McHugh might have *thought* Mort's house was larger, and detached.

Again, McHugh says: "I did not go out of the house again until the following Saturday." In other words, he had hidden himself away for a week following the crime. But this cannot have been true. At the time he was working as a platelayer at Ashton Field Colliery, Little Hulton, and when the police made enquiries there he was recorded as having clocked on for work on the 20th January, 1920—later on the day of the murder.

The police worked hard to find corroboration for McHugh's confession. The story he told was near enough to the truth of what had happened to constitute a thin case, but they wanted to make it stronger. And of course they had the Chief Constable's prior approval to *leave it to the court* to decide what should be done with him. This makes it all the more surprising that when he finally appeared before Bolton County Magistrates on Thursday, 26th November, 1925, no evidence was offered against McHugh for the murder and he was discharged.

Even if pointless now, it is interesting to speculate how the case might have been altered if Lily McHugh and Fanny Shrewsbury had confirmed his confession instead of denying it. Those rows with his wife—those accounts of "fighting" given to his mother, together with the burning of his clothes—the circumstantial value of that kind of evidence would have damned him.

Aside from this, much would have depended on the work being done by the West Riding Constabulary in the field of fingerprint comparison. I have been thwarted in many attempts to find any conclusive reference to this part of the case, but reading between the lines it is fairly evident that McHugh's prints did not agree with any outstanding prints found at the scene. If there had been agreement, then surely the case would have been complete.

The final puzzle concerns the confession written by McHugh. As far as is known, he never withdrew it and he made no claim that it had been obtained under duress. Why, then, was he not arraigned at Assizes and tried on the strength of it? The only feasible explanation is that the police had doubts—and gave him the benefit of them. As it was put to me by Joe Mounsey, until recently Assistant Chief Constable in the Lancashire Constabulary: 'All the information on the file rather gives the lie to the "uncaring" reputation of our forefathers. Obviously McHugh dearly wanted to get himself hanged. It says quite a bit about the integrity of the investigators that he wasn't.'

In a somewhat droll epilogue, McHugh was re-arrested immediately after discharge and ordered by the court to serve imprisonment for one month. This was in execution of a warrant outstanding against him.

It was for arrears of wife maintenance amounting to *two pounds three shillings*.

13

The Manhunt of Dalby Forest
by
PETER N WALKER

In June 1982, a huge and peaceful forest on the North York Moors became the focus of Britain's largest manhunt, with about 800 police officers searching for an armed, cunning and dangerous killer. He was Barry Peter Edwards, also known as Barry Peter Prudom.

He had shot and killed two young North Yorkshire policemen and one civilian gentleman from Lincolnshire, and had shot at and injured a third North Yorkshire policeman. Later, Prudom took two elderly people hostage at Malton as he tried to evade those who sought to bring him to justice. At that time, I was one of those police officers, my role being that of Press Officer with responsibilities for liaising with the press, radio and television during the hunt.

The drama began on Thursday, 17th June 1982 when 29-year-old PC David Haigh of Harrogate was shot dead whilst on routine patrol. He had left Harrogate police station at 7.30 a.m in his official white Ford Fiesta panda car, taking with him some summonses which he intended to serve during his tour of duty. Two hours later, when he failed to respond to radio calls from his colleagues, they began to search for him and shortly before 10 a.m found him lying dead beside his car. The location was a well-known picnic area called Warren Point; it is at Norwood Edge beside the B6451 Otley to Blubberhouses road as it crosses part of the ancient Forest of Knaresborough.

PC Haigh had died from a head wound inflicted at point blank range by a small calibre firearm, probably a .22 pistol. Lying beneath his body was a clipboard upon which he had written "Clive Jones, born 18.10.44, Leeds, n.f.a" and the car registration number KYG 326P.

It seemed that PC Haigh had left his car to interrogate a suspicious person in possession of another vehicle at this place; the young constable had managed to write down those scant particulars before he died. The letters "n.f.a" are an abbreviation for "no fixed address."

The killer had vanished and so had the car, KYG 326P, and an immediate search was commenced. An Incident Room was quickly established at Harrogate Police

Station with Detective Superintendent John Carlton in charge, in the absence (overseas) of the head of North Yorkshire CID, Detective Chief Superintendent Strickland Carter.

A computer check of the vehicle number established that it belonged to a green Citroën 1975 model and later enquiries showed it had been bought from a car dealer in London on 13th January by a man calling himself R.D Carlisle. Carlisle had paid £475 cash and had handed over the money at a London tube station. The dealer could remember the incident and described Carlisle as a man between thirty and thirty-five, clean shaven and well dressed. He had a hold-all full of money, spoke with a northern accent and said he had just come off an oil rig and was returning to his home in the north of England.

As the enquiries got under way, a seventeen-year-old youth came forward to say that he passed Warren Point every day on his motor cycle as he drove to work. As his journey was lengthy, he always stopped there for a rest and on the morning of PC Haigh's murder, he had halted for his customary break. The time was just after 7.30 a.m and he remembered seeing a green Citroën car parked there, with a man asleep in the driving seat. He described the man as being in his thirties with a bulbous nose, dark curly hair, and tanned or swarthy features; he was wearing a light coloured canvas anorak with a hood but the youth saw no more due to the position of the man as he slept in the car. More amazingly, the youth could remember the car number.

The first days produced no other positive leads, but on the Sunday evening following the murder, a farmer at Ledsham near Garforth in West Yorkshire, which is just off the A1 near Selby Fork, decided to take his family out for a meal. However, the June weather was so appalling with rain, wind and mist, that he decided to inspect his fields of ripening wheat. As he entered one field, he noticed car tyre marks leading deep into the crop and so he followed the trail. He discovered that a car had been driven 700 yards into the middle of the large field and then abandoned; it could not be seen from the road due to a natural hillock covered by waist-high wheat. Had the farmer not visited his fields that night, the car might have remained hidden for many weeks.

It was the Citroën KYG 326P, which was removed immediately to the Forensic Science Laboratory at Wetherby for a detailed examination. But where was the driver or the man known as R.D Carlisle?

In an attempt to jog the memories of motorists who had driven past Warren Point on 17th June, it was decided to reconstruct the event exactly one week later, with three panda cars taking three possible routes from Harrogate to the picnic site. Any one of those routes might have been used by PC Haigh. The reconstruction would take place between 6 a.m and 9.30 a.m, during which time passing motorists would be stopped to ask if they could recall anything of that fateful morning, in particular whether anyone had noticed a hurriedly departing green Citroën or the white police car.

Before the reconstruction was staged, however, Detective Superintendent Carlton learned of another killing. On Tuesday, 22nd June, Mr George Luckett, a 52-year-old electrician who lived at Girton near Lincoln, had been shot dead. His wife, Sylvia had also been shot, but she had survived and was able to drag herself to a neighbour's house to call for help. In spite of having a bullet in her head, Mrs Luckett survived. She was able to describe how she and her husband had disturbed a man in the act of stealing their brown Rover saloon; its registration number was VAU 875S and it was now missing. Mr Luckett's death was caused by a .22 bullet, probably fired at close range from a pistol.

At this early stage, there was little to link Mr Luckett's death with that of PC Haigh, although it did become known that on Sunday, 20th June, 75-year-old Mrs Freda Jackson of Blyton Carr near Gainsborough, Lincolnshire, had been bound and gagged by a man who had stolen £4.50 and some food. By chance, a gamekeeper had been patrolling nearby woods some days prior to this attack and had seen a man living rough in a woodland shelter. Beside the shelter, he had noticed a green Citroën car. Its number was KYG 326P. Upon reading about the North Yorkshire murder hunt, the gamekeeper notified the police of his sighting and so the crimes were linked; later, ballistic and other evidence positively confirmed the connection.

The gamekeeper described the man he had seen as being in his early thirties, about 5ft 8ins to 5ft 10ins tall, slim with dark, curly hair. At that time, he'd been wearing jeans, tan shoes, a fawn raincoat, brown cotton gloves and a gold-coloured bracelet, a description which matched that given by Mrs Jackson. The gamekeeper's sighting had been on 11th June.

It seemed that after being seen by the gamekeeper, the suspect had driven to Harrogate, killed PC Haigh and driven back to Ledsham. There he had abandoned the Citroën, then somehow made his way to Gainsborough where he had robbed Mrs Jackson, killed Mr Luckett and escaped in the Lucketts' brown Rover. By Wednesday 24th June, therefore, it was known that a very dangerous character was at large and driving a brown 2.6 Rover car, registration number VAU 875S.

Every police officer in Great Britain was alerted to the dangers of stopping the car and questioning its driver, who was known to have a pistol and to use it at the slightest provocation. All air- and sea-ports were checked, customs points supervised and bus and rail termini watched. By now, the hunt had become a nationwide story, headlined in the newspapers and featured in all news bulletins on radio and television.

Meanwhile, behind the scenes some fine police work had been undertaken and the name of a possible suspect had emerged. For legal reasons, it was inadvisable to release the name to the public because widespread publicity of the case might be seen as likely to prejudice a fair trial of the accused, should he ever appear in court. The prime suspect had come to our notice through the diligence of a police officer in the Summonses and Warrants Department of the West Yorkshire Police at Wakefield.

While sifting through some warrants

which had not been executed, he found one in the name of Barry Peter Edwards, alias Prudom. He was wanted for failing to answer bail on a charge of assaulting a motorist with an iron bar, and the officer noted that Prudom's date of birth was 18.10.1944, and that he had been born in Leeds. It is very easy to give a false name at a moment's notice, but very difficult to give a false date of birth. That date, and the place of birth, coincided with those written down by PC Haigh moments before he died.

Prudom had a long record of petty crime and was described as being 5ft 9ins tall, of proportionate build with brown curly hair, blue eyes and a pale complexion with a somewhat swarthy appearance. He was illegitimate by birth and his mother had committed suicide. These two factors worried him considerably; he had tried to join the TA SAS Volunteer 23rd Regiment in Leeds in 1969, but was rejected as unsuitable. He led a nomadic life, sometimes working on oil rigs and even travelling to America, Canada and the Middle East to seek employment and adventure. He admired the work of the SAS and tried to emulate their lifestyle, living in the wild, practising survival techniques and developing his shooting skills by firing at tin cans. One of his heroes was the Yorkshire survival expert Eddie McGee, author of a book called *No Need to Die—The Real Techniques of Survival* (Compton Books, 1979).

Attempts were made to trace Prudom, if only to eliminate him from the enquiry, and on Thursday, 24th June the reconstruction of PC Haigh's murder took place. The publicity surrounding this was used to bolster an appeal to the public for sightings of Mr Luckett's stolen 2.6 litre Rover, VAU 875S. The very same day, a policeman spotted a brown 2.6 litre Rover car at Primrose Valley Holiday Village on the Yorkshire coast near Filey. The car was empty at the time, and it bore the registration number GYG 344T. This was registered in the name of a company at Pickering in Yorkshire.

As it was a comparatively local car, it was suggested it was legitimately parked at the holiday village. The police, however, had strict orders not to approach any suspect car when they were alone, so further enquiries were made, chiefly because GYG 344T was allocated to a 2.3 litre saloon and the alert officer had noticed that the car bearing those plates was, in fact, a 2.6 litre. It was a small distinction but it did raise doubts in his mind. It was enough to suggest that the car at the holiday village was carrying false number plates.

A contingent of armed officers went to the holiday village to examine it—but the car had gone.

Around 6 p.m that same evening, Thursday, 24th June, PC Ken Oliver of the North Yorkshire Police Dog Section was patrolling Bickley Forest, which adjoins Dalby Forest on the North York Moors, when he noticed a brown Rover car, registration number GYG 344T. He was unarmed and alone, apart from his dog which was in the police dog van. A man suddenly emerged from the Rover and began to fire a handgun at the officer. PC Oliver had no time to release his dog; one shot grazed his nose and several more caused him minor injuries as he desperately tried to escape. His thick uniform helped to save his life—as he sought refuge in a nearby cottage, one shot tore the sleeve of his uniform coat. Miraculously, he was not killed, nor did his assailant pursue him, although he did fire at the police dog—and missed.

Instead, he attacked the police van and ripped out the radio, thus denying PC Oliver any means of calling for immediate help, and then he turned his attention to the Rover. He set fire to it and as the car blazed, the man disappeared into the thick forest of conifers. Later, the handcuffs belonging to the late PC Haigh of Harrogate were found in the burnt-out remains of the Rover.

But PC Oliver had seen the attacker's face.

Later, when he summoned help through some people living in the forest, he was shown a photograph of Barry Peter Prudom and confirmed it was the same person. The police now knew they were seeking a man who could survive in these wild conditions and who was still carrying a gun.

The forest would have to be searched, but that was an impossible task. More than the size of Leeds, some twenty-five square miles in area, the forest comprised rough terrain with millions of trees growing so closely together that it was almost permanently dark beneath the canopy of green. Added to this was the weather, for although it was June, thick mist covered these heights and visibility was reduced to a few yards. Even expert foresters worked in pairs in these conditions, for such is the density of the woodland that all sense of direction can be lost within moments—and the task was to find a man who could disappear at will, even in flat, open countryside. Furthermore, he was armed and he was not afraid to kill upon sight. It was a terrifying prospect.

Help came from all quarters—gamekeepers and forestry workers who were familiar with the intricate network of forestry tracks offered their services; RAF helicopters joined the teams; holiday-makers enjoying the forest were asked to vacate their cottages; the press generated immense publicity—and more than 400 police officers from all parts of the north of England were immediately drafted in with more to follow. Road blocks were established at all the forestry entrances, this alone demanding the services of more than 100 officers, but it was utterly impossible to seal off the entire forest. It was like looking for the proverbial needle in a haystack—but this needle was moving all the time with a gun in his hand. Some members of the public could not appreciate the difficulty of searching this area—some thought it was like looking through a piece of parkland with a copse in the centre—but it would have required thousands of officers all within sight of one another to have completely encircled that forest. Imagine trying to contain the entire city of Leeds, then put forest conditions within that city, then fog—and a gunman.

It is not surprising that the able and experienced Prudom slipped through this huge, loose net.

At 2 p.m on Monday, 27th June, a dirty, bedraggled and tired old man trudged across some fields near the village of Old

Malton. Few people took any notice of him. He carried a shoulder bag from which protruded a slender rod, like a radio aerial, and he wore a fawn coloured cagoule.

He had dark, curly hair and a gaunt thin face with the bones showing through.

When a member of the public rang Malton Police to report this sighting, Sergeant David Winter went to investigate, during which time the old man had gone into Old Malton Post Office to buy some food. When he emerged, Sergeant Winter was outside—and the tramp pulled out a handgun. Sergeant Winter ran for his life, but the tramp pursued him and as the sergeant ran into the grounds of the nearby Gilbertine Priory, now the parish church of St Mary, he was shot three times and died where he fell. His killer vanished into the lush countryside.

The search now concentrated on the fields and woods around Malton and more officers were drafted in, now totalling more than 800. In spite of widespread reports of armed officers, only sixteen carried firearms. Among those who volunteered to help was a man called Eddie McGee, the world-renowned survival expert and author of the very book from which Prudom had learned his skills. Eddie McGee was a trained commando, a parachutist, an expert in karate, judo, aikido and other forms of self-defence, a knife thrower, survival expert and businessman. He had learned tracking skills from the natives of Borneo, Zaire, the Yemen and the Sahara, and had lived with pygmies to study their skills.

He ran an adventure school in the Yorkshire Dales and had a son who was a policeman. Eddie seemed the ideal person to help in the search—the teacher would now be tracking a very dangerous pupil.

Such were Eddie McGee's skills that, from a set of footprints, he could tell the sex of the person who made them, their size, whether they were carrying a load and even whether that load was on their back or front. He could tell whether the person was tired or fresh, whether he or she was injured, whether they were sweating or not and even whether they knew they were being followed. But the police could not arm Mr McGee and any help from him could only be on a voluntary basis, with Mr McGee accepting full responsibility for whatever might happen to him.

Meanwhile, the vast forest and moorland search had been transferred to Malton, normally a quiet market town, and its handsome police station became a bustling centre of activity with mobile canteens, sleeping accommodation, police welfare services, computers and a mass of police equipment and vehicles, plus a helicopter on loan from the London Metropolitan Police. It had the latest heat detection devices and night-sight equipment, a direct contrast to Mr McGee's ancient skills. But in spite of all this equipment, Prudom evaded capture.

All exits from Malton by road, rail and field had been supervised. No cars had been stolen, no food taken from isolated farms or cottages, no sightings of him had been reported...it was known that he was hiding somewhere within the town, perhaps in an outbuilding, perhaps in a disused house. But how does one search an entire town? How does one prevent distress and alarm to the public during such a search?

Mr Kenneth Henshaw, the Chief Constable of North Yorkshire, nursed a private fear that Prudom had gone to earth in someone's house, perhaps having taken the householder hostage, but those fears were never made public, partly because we believed Prudom was listening to a radio set. If he had not taken a hostage, any such suggestion from us might prompt him to do so. We continued to assert our belief that he was still in the town, asking the public to report any sightings, or incidents such as food or transport being stolen.

In fact, the Chief Constable's concern was well-founded. At teatime on the evening of Saturday, 3rd July, Mrs Bessie Johnson, who lived a few hundred yards from the police station in Malton, was clearing pots from her kitchen table when she found a man hiding behind a chair in the dining room. He had entered the house while the door was open and when she was otherwise engaged. At gunpoint, he located Mr Johnson, tied up the pensioners, both in their seventies, and having earlier watched the family's routine, settled down to await the return of their son, Brian.

When Brian came home from work and saw his parents tied up, he ran into the house to help them.

Prudom told him, 'You did the right thing. If you'd run *out,* I'd have shot you.'

Prudom then held the family hostage at gunpoint, bathing his bleeding feet, eating and resting. The family won his confidence and he treated them with sympathy and care, even calling Mr Johnson "Dad". He told them he had no intention of staying—he wanted to kill some more policemen. After eleven hours in the house, he left, intending to kill more officers. He could see the lights of the police station a few yards along the street, beyond the tennis courts. At 3 a.m on the Sunday morning, under cover of darkness, he limped from the house and asked the

Johnsons to give him one full day's start. They were still tied up and could do little else.

Prudom hobbled away and Mr Johnson managed to free himself by 5 a.m, so the family made a pretext of going to bed, switching on the upstairs lights and drawing the curtains in case Prudom was watching their house. In fact, Mr Johnson rang Malton Police. Prudom never reached the police station to carry out his murderous threats. Tired and foot-sore, he arrived at Malton Tennis Courts and Bowling Green and lay down from sheer exhaustion. He took shelter in a derelict shed behind a wall and covered himself with some blue plastic sheeting. It was there that the police, accompanied by Eddie McGee, found him.

By 9 a.m, Prudom had been contained in his lair by three armed officers and repeated calls were made for him to surrender. He refused, firing three shots, two of which were aimed at the officers. Both missed their targets. One shot was returned by the police as a warning. Prudom's third shot hit its target—he killed himself with a shot in the head. In that dramatic way, the hunt ended, but no one can forget the bravery of the officers involved in the search or the trauma experienced by those who suffered at his hands.

To this day, no one knows why Prudom embarked on such a devastating rampage across the north of England and there is still a mystery about the brown Rover car's false number plates. It is not known where he obtained them, nor how he managed to select a registration number which belonged to a car of the same make and colour as the one he had stolen—and one which belonged to a firm so close to his area of operation.

Perhaps the most unusual aspect of the case is that PC David Haig effectively solved his own murder. He did so by writing down Prudom's date and place of birth, and the registration number of his killer's car.

It was a harrowing time for the people of Malton and district, but the case of Barry Peter Edwards, alias Prudom, is now part of our extensive criminal history.

14

Where There's a Will
by
BARBARA WHITEHEAD

Wills, and inheritance thereby, have provided writers of both ordinary novels and crime fiction with one of their most frequent ingredients since the novel, as we know it, began. Missing heirs, claimants to estates who may or may not be the genuine article, murder to ensure that one's inheritance is safe, missing wills, property left to unexpected people, solemn scenes of a seated family waiting with bated breath as the old family solicitor reads out the will...where would we be without them?

Today more people are making wills than ever before, and their consequences are likely to be as amusing, as tragic, as productive of drama as any in previous times, although we are no longer as flowery, as intimate or as personal in our wills as we used to be.

A millionaire recently left a will as terse and lacking in human emotion as a series of business telegrams; but doesn't that give us a world of information in itself about his character? A Yorkshire woman who had made several consecutive wills in favour of her step-son changed her mind, left everything to the Queen's corgis—and then died before she could change her mind again. The step-son was far from pleased.

The idea that a will must be read aloud to the assembled family is mistaken—there is no obligation for it to be read at all—but people telephone the probate offices in their hundreds to ask why a family will has not been read out, and sometimes executors ask if they can come to the probate office to read the will to the relatives, as if a probate office were hallowed ground and in some way gave official standing to such a reading.

What the office does, among other things, is to spot when the wording of a will is not clear, or when after making the will correctly, unauthorised deletions or additions have been made, not properly signed and witnessed. Sometimes also the testator takes the opportunity of will making to say what he really thinks about his relatives, and in the interest of family harmony the solicitor and the probate officer endeavour to soften the expletives; like the will in which the beneficiaries were described as buggers of one variety or another. As they were all built to be rugger forwards or heavyweight boxers it was obviously advisable from the point of view of the more slightly built solicitor to omit the descriptions from the official version...

Anyone interested in writing historical detective stories or thrillers will have a field day with wills. There was the story of Trooper Oldroyd for instance. He was Robert Oldroyd, a clothier from Heckmondwyke in the West Riding of Yorkshire, who joined Black Tom Fairfax's army to fight against King Charles I. After a skirmish he lay mortally wounded in the hamlet of Betton, near Market Drayton, and made his will on the 17th March, 1644, five days before he died. This will was later confiscated by officers of the Royalist army, a surprising action in view of the fact that their detachment had been sent for by Prince Rupert and time must have been pressing—what importance could the will of a dead enemy have at that juncture, one wonders? At the battle of Marston Moor, later in the year, the King was decisively defeated. Matthew Langsker, friend and fellow trooper of Robert Oldroyd, was able to tell the beneficiary of the will, one Wilfred Peele, of the events in Shropshire, and Peele set off for the area. There he persuaded people who knew about the will to testify before a committee at Market Drayton, followed by a formal hearing of his claim at Nantwich; then a new version of the will as it was remembered went with the affidavits to York, where it was proved in October 1644.

This—or a similar—procedure is sometimes still used today, when a will has been lost, or where an oral will has been made, as it often is when men are on active service. The soldier who once told his friend just before they went into action, 'If I die everything is to go to Mary,' had his wishes carried out later when it had been possible to establish who Mary was.

Another soldier who died while on a liaison mission twenty-six hours before war was actually declared in the Falklands posed a problem needing official confirmation that he was on a military mission, otherwise his family would have lost the privileges of financial concessions on court fees, and freedom from inheritance tax, which are due to men dying in war.

Victorian wills provide puzzles and human tragedy. A West Riding will, that of Abraham Greenwood of Dewsbury Moor, proved in January 1841, left money and property to his wife on condition she did not remarry—a common enough clause—but also on condition that she "did not on any account or for any reason whatever permit or suffer my [younger] son Abram Greenwood to reside or dwell or live in the said dwelling house at any time whilst she shall remain my widow." As if this was not enough, the father left eighty pounds a year to Abram on condition that if Abram attempted to raise money on the annuity it should become null and void, and that at all times Abram was to reside somewhere in the country at least 80 miles distant from the township of Dewsbury. The elder son was trustee to see that Abram was furnished out of this annuity "with such maintenance, clothing, and other occasional necessities as he should deem fit for him." For the rest of his life Abram was not to go within eighty miles of his home town; what could he have done to deserve such banishment? A fruitful field for speculation here.

Another will was in the form of a letter, written by a woman to her brother. She was sitting in an isolated cottage on the cliffs of the east coast of Yorkshire; her children were in the grip of an outbreak of typhoid and two of them already lay dead in the cottage; her fisherman husband was away, out on the very stormy sea. Fortunately she was able to find witnesses to her signature, and the letter was later accepted as a valid will.

Executors have greater powers than one might think; they are not obliged to reveal the contents of the will to the family or the beneficiaries, although as wills become public documents (to avoid the possibility of fraud) it is possible to obtain copies of proved wills; not everyone, though, would realise this.

A historical example is that of Ellen Nussey, Charlotte Brontë's closest friend. Her brother Richard left the bulk of his estate to Ellen and her sister Anne, but they were refused knowledge of what was happening to it or the administrative costs being deducted from it, and five years after his death were appealing to the executor to allow them some money from the estate, and complaining that he was investing the capital in foreign Railway Bonds against their wishes. Unfortunately he was within his rights.

In this century the executors to a substantial estate were left an allowance in the will of some hundreds for every month the will remained unsettled; month after month they met over a lavish lunch with the best cigars and wine, only to decide reluctantly that they were unable at that point to expedite matters further, and there was nothing for it but to pocket their allowance and go home again. This went on from the twenties into the thirties, over a period of some eleven years.

Wills can be comic too. There was the man who left his budgerigar to his wife, as she was the only person who could out-talk the bird. Another man left instructions that his hearse and mourners were to stop at a certain public house on their journey. The company was to go inside for a drink, for which the money was provided, and they were to bring out a pint of beer and pour it over his coffin.

Don't let us think wills and inheritances as motives for fictional action are outmoded or old-fashioned; times change but people do not, and we are not much different from the cave woman who murdered her mother-in-law in order to inherit her string of beads.

15

A Reasonable Doubt
by
DOUGLAS WYNN

Henry Dobson saw something out of the corner of his eye. He had farmed High Grange for over thirty years and knew all the fields like the back of his hand. From where he was standing, in the middle of a field, half-way between his farm and the village of Wolviston, in County Durham, it looked as if there was something not quite right in one of them. He turned his head and saw that what had caught his eye was a dark blob. It was on the ploughed land beside a farm track, some 150 yards away.

A cold wind blew across the field, bringing with it a hint of January snow. Farmer Dobson shivered and drew his coat closer around him and looked again at the dark shape. He knew it shouldn't be there.

He had been taking a short cut to the village, had branched off the main farm track which joined up with the road, and had gone across the fields. But now he retraced his steps to rejoin the track. And in his heart there was a terrible foreboding.

The long farm path, just about wide enough to take a vehicle and with a grass verge at each side, was raised some two feet above the ploughed land on one side and had a hedge on the other. The farmer walked along it, fearing what he would find, yet knowing that he must find out what the dark shape was. After some time, he realised that he had gone too far. He had to retrace his steps.

Then he found it.

All his fears were confirmed. It was the body of his wife.

She had left the farmhouse late in the afternoon of the previous day to walk to the village. When she did not return in the evening he supposed that she must have caught a bus to Newcastle, some 30 miles to the North, where their daughter lived. And since in those days—this was January, 1938—phones were not common in remote farmhouses, he was not unduly worried that she hadn't heard from her by the next day.

The body, almost hidden by the grass verge at one side of the track, lay a couple of feet down on the ploughed land. Through tear-misted eyes he could see that

313

she was quite dead. Lying on her back, with her head towards the farmhouse, her face was swollen and discoloured and there was blood around her mouth. He might have assumed that she had died from some kind of seizure, but her clothes were pulled up and her legs splayed apart in the classic position of rape. Mrs Dobson had been sixty-seven years old.

After allowing the tears to subside and walking round the body, Henry Dobson ran down the farm track to the main road, and thence into Wolviston, looking for help.

He eventually met Police Constable John Chapman in the street. 'Come quickly!' shouted Dobson. 'My wife's been murdered!'

As they were hurrying back they were lucky enough to be overtaken by Doctor James Craven, who was driving through the village in his car. They stopped him and all three drove out to the gate where the farm track met the road. Leaving the car they went 50 yards up the path to where the body lay.

After the medical man had been examining Mrs Dobson for some time the constable spoke. 'How long has she been dead, doctor?'

'Several hours I would say, as a preliminary guess. At least four or five, but not more than twenty-four.'

PC Chapman went to report to his superiors and soon several other policemen appeared on the scene.

Superintendent George Kirkup was in charge. He was assisted by Detective Sergeant Edward Foster, who made plaster casts of the footprints around the body, and Detective Sergeant Ralph Lee, who took photographs. They made a careful search round the body and in the surrounding fields.

Mrs Dobson's false teeth were found some little distance from the body, knocked out presumably by vicious blows to her face. Her handbag and a shopping bag were found close by and there were footprints as well as distinct marks in the soil where she had pushed herself backwards in a vain attempt to get away from her attacker.

On the grass verge, just opposite the body, was a depression from the wheel of a lorry.

The police began taking statements and late in the afternoon the body was removed to West Hartlepool mortuary.

The autopsy was conducted by Dr Cookson, the pathologist at Sunderland Royal Infirmary. He found that the left eye was black and there was bruising on the left side of the jaw, which indicated that the assailant had been right-handed.

There was ample evidence of rape. Injuries to the vagina suggested forcible penetration and the presence of semen was evidence of recent sexual intercourse. The pubic hair was also matted.

The cause of death soon became obvious. There were two stab wounds, one just above the left breast, and the other in the left side of the throat. The pathologist thought that, although both had probably been delivered with a small-bladed knife, probably no more than a pen-knife, either might have been fatal.

The thrust in the throat had cut the left jugular vein and would have resulted in massive internal bleeding. Death would have occurred in a matter of minutes.

The picture that was emerging suggested that Mrs Dobson had been attacked on her way down the farm track. She had either been dragged or had stumbled onto the ploughed land where the rape, which had occurred before death, had taken place. She had then died from the knife wounds.

The time of her death turned out to be important but the evidence about it was confusing.

Henry Dobson spoke to Detective Sergeant Foster.

'I had tea with my wife about 3.15,' said the farmer, 'and during the meal she told me she was going out. I asked her what time she expected to be back and she said about six.'

'And that was the last time you saw your wife?' asked Foster.

'No. I later saw her in the farm yard. She was dressed in her going-out clothes.'

'Was she carrying anything?'

The farmer scratched his head. 'Let me see now. She was carrying a handbag I think.'

'Nothing else?'

Again there was a pause. 'No,' said Dobson slowly. 'She said goodbye to me and went off along the farm track.'

'What time would that be, sir?'

Dobson chewed his lower lip in thought. 'That would be...let me think now. It was getting pretty dark, so that would put it at about 4.30.'

That same afternoon a threshing machine arrived at the farm to start work the following morning. The operator was Bertram Smith and he was accompanied by two helpers.

He was also interviewed by Detective Foster.

'We arrived at High Grange,' reported Smith, 'at about half past three and got the machine ready for the morning.'

The policeman made a note in his notebook. 'What time did you leave?'

'It must have been 4.30.'

'Are you sure of the time?'

It was Smith's turn to think. 'Yes, because I heard a local factory buzzer go and that's always at 4.30.'

Foster looked at Smith. 'Now think very carefully. Did any of you see anything or anyone as you went along the track?'

Smith shook his head decisively. 'No. We certainly never saw Mrs Dobson.'

Foster nodded. 'What did you do then?'

'When we got to the main road, we rode into Wolviston.'

Now, either Mrs Dobson had already been killed when the three men pushed their cycles down the farm path—which seems extremely unlikely—or the farmer made a mistake about the time he saw her leave. Since the local policeman reported that lighting-up time that day was between 4.30 and 4.45 it is very likely that when Dobson saw her leave it was after 4.30, since he said it was getting pretty dark.

He also saw her leave with only a handbag, whereas when she was found she had with her a shopping bag as well. This could mean that she went back into the house, after Dobson saw her start out, to collect the shopping bag.

The police also received some vital information from Percy Swales, the driver of a Bedford cattle truck. Dobson had been to Sedgefield market on the morning of the murder and bought eight pigs.

Swales told Detective Sergeant Foster, 'I left Sedgefield with the pigs at five o'clock and got to the farm at 5.30 or thereabouts.'

Henry Dobson afterwards confirmed this.

'It was dark of course,' continued the lorry driver, 'and as I swung into the farm track the headlights picked out the figure of a man standing about fifty yards away. He was standing with his arms above his head and was just to the right of the track. As the lights hit him he dropped to the plough.'

'Could you see what he was wearing?' asked Foster.

'Not very well. He looked as if he had on a bluish smock, like farm workers wear, and a brownish coat. And he might have had leggings on.'

'Did he have anything on his head?'

'A cap,' replied Swales.

He then described driving up the path with the headlights cutting a swathe through the darkness. When he approached the spot where the man had been he saw ahead of him a bicycle on the left-hand verge with its back wheel sticking out over the track. He had to swerve to avoid it and the rear offside wheel of his lorry went up over the grass.

'I stopped the Bedford,' he said. 'Then I could see the faint outline of a man on my right lying on the plough, but I couldn't see his face. I spoke to him. "What's the game here?" He said: "I'm all right. I've had one over the nine. Drive on." '

'Did you recognise his voice?'

The lorry driver thought for a minute. 'No, but it was definitely a local accent.'

Swales' assistant Thomas Nelson was sitting beside him in the cab and confirmed his story. Nelson was also closer to the bicycle as they passed and described it as a racing cycle with dropped handlebars.

Since the mark in the turf where the back wheel of the lorry had mounted the verge was exactly at the position where the body was later found, there seems little doubt that the man that the lorry men saw was the murderer. The murder must have been committed, therefore, between 4.30, when Bertram Smith and his men pushed their cycles down the path, and 5.30 or a little after. It also means that the murderer could not have left the scene until 5.30.

Apart from supplying the police with information about when his wife left the farm, Henry Dobson also had an interesting story to tell. When he was asked by Sergeant Foster if he had any enemies or could think of anyone who might have had a grudge against Mrs Dobson, he scratched his head.

'There's the Hoolhouses,' he remarked. 'The family used to live in the hind's cottage on my farm. That would be, let me see, about five years ago. I found they were watering the milk and I ordered them out. Told them never to come back. They went to live in Haverton Hill I believe.'

'And you think they might hold a grudge that long?'

'Well, the young boy, Robert, was only about fifteen at the time, so he'd be now about twenty. I know that he does farm work, when he can get it, around here. And I do know that he sometimes hires out to Bert Smith on the thresher. He'd know that Bert would be coming yesterday and at what time. Suppose he'd called to see if he could get any work? He'd almost certainly meet Mrs Dobson coming down the track. If she recognised him she would have ordered him off the property. He might have lost his temper and...'

It seems that this idea also occurred to Bertram Smith, who already knew about the murder, having been at the farm when the body was discovered. That same day—the day after the murder—he met Robert Hoolhouse in Haverton Hill, a village a couple of miles east of

Billingham and about three miles south east of Wolviston. He came upon the tall, spectacled figure of the young man, who was wearing his usual uniform of blue overalls and a brown jacket, outside the newspaper shop at about six o'clock in the evening.

Hoolhouse was looking at placards announcing: "Wolviston Woman's Murder".

'Now then, young Hoolhouse,' he said. 'Why didn't you come to see me at Wolviston on Tuesday? Don't you want any more work on the thresher?'

According to Smith, Hoolhouse looked decidedly nervous. 'I was in Wolviston on Tuesday,' muttered the young man, but offered no further explanation.

'You've got some scratches on your cheek,' pursued Smith. 'How did you get those?'

Hoolhouse cleared his throat. 'Fell off my bike.'

'How did you do that?'

To the threshing machine operator the young man looked exceedingly jumpy. He didn't seem to be able to keep still and kept shuffling from one foot to the other. Eventually he said: 'Put my front brake on too quick and went over the handlebars.'

'Hmm. Any other injuries?'

'I've hurt my right shoulder as well.' He rubbed it, as if to indicate that it still hurt.

Smith stared at him long and hard. 'You certainly look to me as if you've had a shock. That's for certain.'

'Yes, and it'll be a bit before I get over it.'

'I'm sure it will,' said the operator slowly.

He nodded towards the placards. 'What do you think of that?'

In Smith's subsequent account of the conversation, the young man looked round wildly and it seemed as if he might run away. Smith stepped up close. 'Horrible murder, wasn't it?'

He looked up at the tall young man, who nodded his head, but said nothing. 'How did you hear about it, then?' pressed the operator.

'Arthur Nicholson, the postman, told me.'

While this was going on the pair had been watched by another man. Herbert Collins was an ex-policeman, who now did occasional farm work. He sometimes worked for Smith and he knew Hoolhouse. He had heard most of the conversation and when the operator turned to go into the paper shop Collins stepped forward and took the young man's arm.

'When did you say you had the accident with your bike?'

Hoolhouse turned towards him. 'Ten

o'clock,' he mumbled.

'You mean ten o'clock at night?'

'No, ten in the morning.'

Collins shifted his ground. 'Were you in Wolviston last night?'

Hoolhouse glanced down at his boots. Then he looked up. 'Yes. And I've been there again today.'

'The police will want to question you,' said Collins and watched the young man's face go pale.

'I bloody well hope not!'

'Oh, yes,' said the ex-policeman with obvious enjoyment. 'You'll have to tell them everything you've been up to. Who you've seen. All that.' Then he continued slowly, watching Hoolhouse's face carefully. 'Your family used to work for Mr Dobson, didn't they?'

'That was a long time ago.'

When Hoolhouse had gone and Smith had come out of the paper shop, the two men discussed the situation and at ten o'clock that night they went to the police station in Stockton, the main one in the area. They told the police of their suspicions and reported their conversations with the young man. The result of this was that at 1.15 in the morning, Police Constable Joseph Hodgson knocked on the door of the little house in Pickering Street, Haverton Hill, where Robert Hoolhouse lived with his family.

A sleepy Robert Hoolhouse was told to get dressed and was then taken to Haverton Hill police station, where he was questioned by Detective Sergeant Foster.

Hoolhouse made a statement in which he said that he had stayed at home until about 12.30 p.m on Tuesday, the day of the murder. Then he cycled to Wolviston and visited a young lady, a Miss Lax, who lived there with her aunt, Miss Husband. He stayed until about 3.30 then left and cycled home. One of the routes to Haverton Hill was through Billingham and this would have taken him right past the entrance to the farm track leading to High Grange. The other and probably slightly shorter route was through a little village called Cowpen Bewley. He claimed to have gone this way and to have arrived home at just after 4 o'clock.

If this was true he couldn't possibly have committed the murder, which didn't take place until after 4.30.

He also said that on the way back home he came off his cycle, scraping his right cheek and hurting his right shoulder.

The same night, his statement continued, he left home at 6.30 to take Miss Lax to the pictures. He caught a bus to Billingham and there changed to one for Wolviston, arriving at just after seven. Then he and

Miss Lax boarded a bus to Billingham, where they went to the second-house pictures and saw the film "Between Two Flags".

After the programme he put Miss Lax on the bus for Wolviston and went home himself, arriving at 11.30.

On the following day he again cycled to Wolviston in the afternoon, arriving at 1.45 and staying, talking to Miss Husband and Miss Lax, for about half an hour before going home, which he reached by 3 o'clock.

He admitted seeing Smith and Collins by the paper shop at 6 o'clock, but denied telling Smith that he was looking for him to join his machine or that anything was said about the police wanting to see him.

He agreed that he had been employed by Mr Dobson five years ago, but said that the last time he had seen Mrs Dobson was just before the previous Christmas when he had gone to High Grange looking for work.

While the statement was being taken the police went back to Pickering Street and returned with a raincoat belonging to Hoolhouse. Then, when the statement was finished and he had signed it, he was asked to take off his clothes.

The police officers saw no sign of stiffness in his right shoulders, as he removed his clothes, and there was no bruising. They did see, however, definite scratch marks on his face.

At about seven o'clock in the morning Hoolhouse was taken to Stockton Police Station. There he was seen by Superintendent Kirkup.

'This statement of yours,' said the Superintendent, tapping the sheaf of papers on the desk in front of him. 'It's not correct is it?'

'Of course it is.'

'Well, you may be interested to learn that we have contacted the people you mention, Miss Husband and Miss Lax, and they say that you didn't get to the house in Wolviston until 3.30. You stayed about an hour, so you must have left at 4.30, not at 3.30 as you say in your statement.'

The young man looked puzzled. 'I suppose I must have made a mistake,' he said slowly. 'If they say I was there later.'

'Do you wish to alter your statement?'

'Yes, I think I'd better.'

Bloodstains were found on the clothes which Hoolhouse had been wearing when he was taken to the police station. A handkerchief discovered in the pocket of the overalls was found to be heavily bloodstained. Both wrist bands of the brown check shirt he was wearing were also stained with blood as were the bottom of the sleeves of the jacket corresponding to the stains on the shirt cuffs.

All these proved to be of Group II of the Moss classification, corresponding to the modern Group A. It was subsequently discovered that the murdered woman's blood was also Group II. When asked about these stains Hoolhouse said that he had cut himself shaving.

Some small bloodstains were also found on his trousers, between the fly buttons, and on the overalls in the same position, but these proved too small to determine the group.

When the committal proceedings began, a document was handed to the police, from his solicitors, stating that Hoolhouse did not wish to submit to a blood test. And, since it was his right in law to do this, none was taken.

A single hair was found on the blood-stained handkerchief, which it was afterwards proved could not have come from Hoolhouse's head but which might have come from the head of Mrs Dobson. And pubic hair found on the front flap of the prisoner's shirt might also have come from Mrs Dobson.

A knife found in the pocket of a waistcoat belonging to Hoolhouse was described by the pathologist as being fully capable of inflicting the wounds found on the murdered woman.

Robert Hoolhouse was tried at the Leeds Assizes in March 1938. In the prosecution case, the evidence of Miss Lax and Miss Husband put the prisoner very near to the farm track at the time when Mrs Dobson would have come down it. His first statement gave him an alibi for the time of the murder which was afterwards shown to be false. He had blood and hairs on him which could have come from Mrs Dobson and he had scratches on his face which might have been inflicted by a woman fighting for her life. He also owned a knife which could have killed her and a cycle of the type described by the lorry driver's mate.

But, as the judge was to point out, it was circumstantial evidence which might just as easily indicate that he did not commit the crime.

The dropped-handlebar cycle, which Hoolhouse owned, was a very common type and many young men had similar machines. The same could be said of his knife. In addition, the only trace of blood on it was a very small amount in the thumb nail recess on the blade. The prosecution claimed that the knife had been thoroughly cleaned.

The prisoner explained the scratches on

his face by saying he had fallen from his bicycle and the prosecution were able to bring no medical evidence to show that they could not have been caused in this way. And when it is realised that Mrs Dobson, when found, was actually wearing woollen gloves, the strength of this evidence is seriously weakened.

The blood and hairs really should have been the strongest link in the chain of evidence against Hoolhouse. But the expert who testified on the hairs for the prosecution, Professor Tryhorn, was asked: 'Though you found many characteristics in common between the samples, you would not be prepared to swear that any of these hairs had come from any particular person?' And the professor had to agree. 'No, I would not,' he said. 'It is impossible with hair.'

And because Hoolhouse lived in a small house in close proximity to at least one woman it is not really surprising that hair which was not his own could be found on his clothes.

A similar argument could be used about the bloodstains. Hoolhouse's casual work as a farm worker, particularly his employment on the threshing machine, might very well bring him into contact with other people's blood, which could possibly have got on to his clothes.

And a significant fact about his clothes was that although there was some blood, even on the flies, there was no semen. Mrs Dobson had undoubtedly been raped. Spermatozoa was discovered in her vagina and her pubic hairs were matted with it, but none was discovered on the prisoner's clothes.

The prosecution made great play with the fact that Hoolhouse, in his first statement, gave himself an alibi for the time of the murder by saying that he was at home. And that this indicated, they said, that he must have known what time the murder had been committed.

But it is significant that although he apparently lied about the time he was in Wolviston he also named witnesses who could prove that he was lying. It is far more likely that he made a genuine mistake about the times he arrived and left the two women.

Even if he lied deliberately, under the circumstances it is not altogether surprising. Having been quizzed by Bertram Smith and Herbert Collins on the day after the murder, he must have realised that they suspected him. If he was innocent he would still be quite likely to panic, knowing that he had been in the vicinity of High Grange the previous afternoon. When the police descended on him only a few hours later, his first inclination might have been to say that he had spent as little time in Wolviston as possible.

The fact which might be thought to point to his guilt was his refusal to take a blood test. If he was innocent, it was claimed, he would know that the blood stains were his own and would be the same group as Mrs Dobson. But if his blood group turned out to be different from Mrs Dobson how would he explain them?

In fact Mrs Dobson's blood group is held by nearly half the population of this country, so although the bloodstains on his clothes were of that group it doesn't necessarily follow that they belonged to Mrs Dobson, even if they were a different group from his own.

Other evidence involved footprints. There was a clear set of prints from Mr Dobson's gum boots, where he walked round the body. But one of his heel marks had crossed another, larger, footprint. Detective Sergeant Foster had taken plaster casts of the print and he gave it as his opinion, in court, that the larger print had been made before the farmer's heel print became superimposed upon it. The larger print might well have been made by the murderer and Foster had to agree that it bore no resemblance to the accused's footprints.

Another point in Hoolhouse's favour was that the description Percy Swales gave of the man he saw on the ploughed land made no mention of him wearing spectacles, which the accused man did. And the headlights of a lorry would surely have been reflected strongly from the lenses had the man been wearing them.

Hoolhouse's counsel, Mr Arthur Morley K.C, obviously felt that the evidence against his client was weak, for at the end of the prosecution case he submitted that there was no case which could safely be left to the jury. Mr Justice Wrottesley, however, disagreed, whereupon Mr Morley called no witnessess for the defence.

No doubt the defence counsel had his reasons for this, but it seems a curious decision, especially in view of the possible evidence from Hoolhouse's father. In the accused's second statement he declared that he was home by five o'clock. If that were true he could not have been the man seen by Percy Swales and Thomas Nelson when they delivered the pigs at 5.30. Mr Frederick Hoolhouse was in the house when his son arrived home and could presumably have confirmed the time. The fact that he was not called by the prosecution seems to indicate that his evidence was not detrimental to Hoolhouse. However, he was not called by the defence.

Robert Hoolhouse was not called to give evidence on his own behalf either.

Prosecuting counsel, Mr Paley Scott K.C, then made his final speech to the jury. This was followed by Mr Morley's speech for the defence. Since he had called no witnesses he was allowed the final word. He ended his speech with these words to the jury: 'Can any one of you say: "I am satisfied that this man is guilty and that the case has been proved?" I submit that you cannot.'

Mr Justice Wrottesley gave a very fair summing up. All the evidence, he pointed out, was circumstantial. On the one hand it was consistent with Hoolhouse being the murderer, but it was also consistent with his not having committed the crime. And he went on to tell the jury that they must ask themselves: ' "Do all these circumstances, suspicious though they are...do they convince me beyond all reasonable doubt, beyond the possibility of mistake, that this young man murdered that old lady?" If they do, your duty is plain, and you will not shrink from it. But if you think that all it amounts to is this—that very likely that young fellow did it, but we cannot be certain—if that is the frame of mind you are left in, then your duty is equally plain, and it is to say "not guilty".'

By all accounts most people in court expected that the verdict would be "not guilty". Hoolhouse's mother and father had a taxi waiting to take him home. But the jury, which did not have a woman on it, was out for four hours, which sounds as if there was a good deal of deliberation. When they filed back they did not look at the prisoner. The foreman stood, his face pale, and pronounced the one word: 'Guilty'.

A hush fell on the court as the judge reached for the black cap. During the sentencing he did not, as many do, say that he agreed with the verdict.

An appeal was made on the grounds that the judge should not have allowed the case to go before the jury, and it was heard in May. It was rejected. Over 14,000 people signed a petition to the Home Secretary for a reprieve. This was also rejected.

Robert Hoolhouse was hanged in Durham Gaol on May 26th, 1938.

The case caused no sensation in the national newspapers. It was the year of the Munich agreement between Chamberlain and Hitler and all through the summer there were rumours of an impending war with Germany. Gas masks were issued. London parks were dug up for air-raid shelters. Nobody bothered about an obscure murder up North.

And yet there are grave doubts about this case. The evidence on which Hoolhouse was convicted was very slim. Even the prosecuting counsel admitted in court: 'Of course this is a case of very much less evidence than one usually finds...' Hoolhouse may have been the murderer, but did the prosecution prove it? Wasn't he, like any other person accused of a crime, entitled to be presumed innocent until he was proved guilty, beyond all reasonable doubt? And in this case, wasn't there a reasonable doubt?